THE
WORLD'S
ONE HUNDRED
BEST SHORT STORIES

[IN TEN VOLUMES]

GRANT OVERTON
EDITOR - IN - CHIEF

VOLUME NINE
GHOSTS

FUNK & WAGNALLS COMPANY
NEW YORK AND LONDON

CONTENTS

THE WORLD'S 100 BEST
SHORT STORIES

THE RED ROOM

By H. G. WELLS

"I can assure you," said I, "that it will take a very tangible ghost to frighten me." And I stood up before the fire with my glass in my hand.

"It is your own choosing," said the man with the withered arm, and glanced at me askance.

"Eight-and-twenty years," said I, "I have lived, and never a ghost have I seen as yet."

The old woman sat staring hard into the fire, her pale eyes wide open. "Ay," she broke in, "and eight-and-twenty years you have lived, and never seen the likes of this house, I reckon. There's a many things to see, when one's still but eight-and-twenty." She swayed her head from side to side. "A many things to see and sorrow for." I suspected these old people were trying to enhance the spectral terrors of their house by this droning insistence. I put down my empty glass on the table, and, looking about the room, caught a glimpse of myself abbreviated and broadened to an impossible sturdiness, in the queer old mirror beside the china cupboard. "Well," I said, "if I see anything to-night, I shall be so much the wiser. For I come to the business with an open mind."

"It's your own choosing," said the man with the withered arm once more.

I heard the faint sound of a stick and a shambling step on the flags in the passage outside. The door creaked on its hinges as a second old man entered, more bent, more wrinkled, more aged even than the first. He supported himself by the help of a crutch, his eyes were covered by a shade, and his lower lip, half averted, hung pale and pink from his decaying yellow teeth. He made straight for an armchair on the opposite side of the table, sat down clumsily, and began to cough. The man with the withered hand gave the newcomer a short glance of positive dislike; the old woman took no notice of his arrival, but remained with her eyes fixed steadily on the fire.

"I said—it's your own choosing," said the man with the withered hand, when the coughing had ceased for a while.

"It's my own choosing," I answered.

The man with the shade became aware of my presence for the first time, and threw his head back for a moment, and sidewise, to see me. I caught a momentary glimpse of his eyes, small and bright and inflamed. Then he began to cough and splutter again.

"Why don't you drink?" said the man with the withered arm, pushing the beer toward him. The man with the shade poured out a glassful with a shaking hand, that splashed half as much again on the deal table. A monstrous shadow of him crouched upon the wall, and mocked his action as he poured and drank. I must confess I had scarcely expected these grotesque custodians. There is, to my mind, something inhuman in senility, something crouching and atavistic; the human qualities seem to drop from old people insensi-

bly day by day. The three of them made me feel
uncomfortable with their gaunt silences, their bent
carriage, their evident unfriendliness to me and to one
another. And that night, perhaps, I was in the mood
for uncomfortable impressions. I resolved to get
away from their vague foreshadowings of the evil
things upstairs.

"If," said I, "you will show me to this haunted room
of yours, I will make myself comfortable there."

The old man with the cough jerked his head back
so suddenly that it startled me, and shot another glance
of his red eyes at me from out the darkness under the
shade, but no one answered me. I waited a minute,
glancing from one to the other. The old woman stared
like a dead body, glaring into the fire with lack-luster
eyes.

"If," I said, a little louder, "if you will show me to
this haunted room of yours, I will relieve you from
the task of entertaining me."

"There's a candle on the slab outside the door," said
the man with the withered hand, looking at my feet
as he addressed me. "But if you go to the Red Room
to-night—"

"This night of all nights!" said the old woman,
softly.

"—You go alone."

"Very well," I answered, shortly, "and which way
do I go?"

"You go along the passage for a bit," said he, nodding his head on his shoulder at the door, "until you
come to a spiral staircase; and on the second landing is a door covered with green baize. Go through
that, and down the long corridor to the end, and the
Red Room is on your left up the steps."

"Have I got that right?" I said, and repeated his directions.

He corrected me in one particular.

"And you are really going?" said the man with the shade, looking at me again for the third time with that queer, unnatural tilting of the face.

"This night of all nights!" whispered the old woman.

"It is what I came for," I said, and moved toward the door. As I did so, the old man with the shade rose and staggered round the table, so as to be closer to the others and to the fire. At the door I turned and looked at them, and saw they were all close together, dark against the firelight, staring at me over their shoulders, with an intent expression on their ancient faces.

"Good-night," I said, setting the door open.

"It's your own choosing," said the man with the withered arm.

I left the door wide open until the candle was well alight, and then I shut them in, and walked down the chilly, echoing passage.

I must confess that the oddness of these three old pensioners in whose charge her ladyship had left the castle, and the deep-toned, old-fashioned furniture of the housekeeper's room, in which they foregathered, had affected me curiously in spite of my effort to keep myself at a matter-of-fact phase. They seemed to belong to another age, an older age, an age when things spiritual were indeed to be feared, when common sense was uncommon, an age when omens and witches were credible, and ghosts beyond denying. Their very existence, thought I, is spectral; the cut of their clothing, fashions born in dead brains; the ornaments and conveniences in the room about them even are ghostly—

the thoughts of vanished men, which still haunt rather than participate in the world of to-day. And the passage I was in, long and shadowy, with a film of moisture glistening on the wall, was as gaunt and cold as a thing that is dead and rigid. But with an effort I sent such thoughts to the right-about. The long, drafty subterranean passage was chilly and dusty, and my candle flared and made the shadows cower and quiver. The echoes rang up and down the spiral staircase, and a shadow came sweeping up after me, and another fled before me into the darkness overhead. I came to the wide landing and stopped there for a moment listening to a rustling that I fancied I heard creeping behind me, and then, satisfied of the absolute silence, pushed open the unwilling baize-covered door and stood in the silent corridor.

The effect was scarcely what I expected, for the moonlight, coming in by the great window on the grand staircase, picked out everything in vivid black shadow or reticulated silvery illumination. Everything seemed in its proper position; the house might have been deserted on the yesterday instead of twelve months ago. There were candles in the sockets of the sconces, and whatever dust had gathered on the carpets or upon the polished flooring was distributed so evenly as to be invisible in my candlelight. A waiting stillness was over everything. I was about to advance, and stopped abruptly. A bronze group stood upon the landing hidden from me by a corner of the wall; but its shadow fell with marvelous distinctness upon the white paneling, and gave me the impression of some one crouching to waylay me. The thing jumped upon my attention suddenly. I stood rigid for half a moment, perhaps. Then, with my hand in the pocket that held the revolver, I advanced, only to discover a Ganymede and Eagle, glistening in the moonlight. That incident for a time restored my nerve, and a dim porcelain Chinaman on a buhl table, whose head rocked as I passed, scarcely startled me.

The door of the Red Room and the steps up to it were in a shadowy corner. I moved my candle from side to side in order to see clearly the nature of the recess in which I stood, before opening the door. Here it was, thought I, that my predecessor was found, and the memory of that story gave me a sudden twinge of apprehension. I glanced over my shoulder at the black Ganymede in the moonlight, and opened the door of the Red Room rather hastily, with my face half turned to the pallid silence of the corridor.

I entered, closed the door behind me at once, turned the key I found in the lock within, and stood with the candle held aloft surveying the scene of my vigil, the great Red Room of Lorraine Castle, in which the young Duke had died; or rather in which he had begun his dying, for he had opened the door and fallen headlong down the steps I had just ascended. That had been the end of his vigil, of his gallant attempt to conquer the ghostly tradition of the place, and never, I thought, had apoplexy better served the ends of superstition. There were other and older stories that clung to the room, back to the half-incredible beginning of it all, the tale of a timid wife and the tragic end that came to her husband's jest of frightening her. And looking round that huge shadowy room with its black window bays, its recesses and alcoves, its dusty brown-red hangings and dark gigantic furniture, one could well understand the legends that had sprouted in its black corners, its germinating darknesses. My candle was a little tongue of light in the vastness of the chamber; its rays failed to pierce to the opposite end of the room, and left an ocean of dull red mystery and suggestion, sentinel shadows and watching darknesses beyond its island of light. And the stillness of desolation brooded over it all.

I must confess some impalpable quality of that ancient room disturbed me. I tried to fight the feeling down. I resolved to make a systematic examination of the place, and so, by leaving nothing to the imagination, dispel the fanciful suggestions of the obscurity before they obtained a hold upon me. After satisfying myself of the fastening of the door, I began to walk round the room, peering round each article of furniture, tucking up the valances of the bed and opening its curtains wide. In one place there was a distinct echo to my footsteps, the noises I made seemed so little that they enhanced rather than broke the silence of the place. I pulled up the blinds and examined the fastenings of the several windows. Attracted by the fall of a particle of dust, I leaned forward and looked up the blackness of the wide chimney. Then, trying to preserve my scientific attitude of mind, I walked round and began tapping the oak paneling for any secret opening, but I desisted before reaching the alcove. I saw my face in a mirror—white.

There were two big mirrors in the room, each with a pair of sconces bearing candles, and on the mantelshelf, too, were candles in china candlesticks. All these I lit one after the other. The fire was laid—an unexpected consideration from the old housekeeper— and I lit it, to keep down any disposition to shiver, and when it was burning well I stood round with my back to it and regarded the room again. I had pulled up a chintz-covered armchair and a table to form a kind of barricade before me. On this lay my revolver, ready to hand. My precise examination had done me a little good, but I still found the remoter darkness of the place and its perfect stillness too stimulating for the imagination. The echoing of the stir and crackling of the fire was no sort of comfort to me. The shadow in the alcove at the end of the room began to display that undefinable quality of a presence, that odd suggestion of a lurking living thing that comes so easily in silence and solitude. And to reassure myself, I walked with a candle into it and satisfied myself that there was nothing tangible there. I stood that candle upon the floor of the alcove and left it in that position.

By this time I was in a state of considerable nervous tension, altho to my reason there was no adequate cause for my condition. My mind, however, was perfectly clear. I postulated quite unreservedly that nothing supernatural could happen, and to pass the time I began stringing some rimes together, Ingoldsby fashion, concerning the original legend of the place. A few I spoke aloud, but the echoes were not pleasant. For the same reason I also abandoned, after a time, a conversation with myself upon the impossibility of ghosts and haunting. My mind reverted to the three old and distorted people downstairs, and I tried to keep it upon that topic.

The somber reds and grays of the room troubled me; even with its seven candles the place was merely dim. The light in the alcove flaring in a draft, and the fire flickering, kept the shadows and penumbra perpetually shifting and stirring in a noiseless flighty dance. Casting about for a remedy, I recalled the wax candles I had seen in the corridor, and, with a slight effort, carrying a candle and leaving the door open, I walked out into the moonlight, and presently returned with as many as ten. These I put in the various knick-knacks of china with which the room was sparsely adorned, and lit and placed them where the shadows had lain deepest, some on the floor, some in the window recesses, arranging and rearranging them until at last my seventeen candles were so placed that not an inch of the room but had the direct light of at least one of them. It occurred to me that when the ghost came I could warn him not to trip over them. The room was now quite brightly illuminated. There was something very cheering and reassuring in these little silent streaming flames, and to notice their steady diminution of length offered me an occupation and gave me a reassuring sense of the passage of time.

Even with that, however, the brooding expectation of the vigil weighed heavily enough upon me. I stood watching the minute hand of my watch creep towards midnight.

Then something happened in the alcove. I did not see the candle go out, I simply turned and saw that the darkness was there, as one might start and see the unexpected presence of a stranger. The black shadow had sprung back to its place. "By Jove," said I aloud, recovering from my surprize, "that draft's a strong one"; and taking the matchbox from the table, I walked across the room in a leisurely manner to relight the corner again. My first match would not strike, and as I succeeded with the second, something seemed to blink on the wall before me. I turned my head involuntarily and saw that the two candles on the little table by the fireplace were extinguished. I rose at once to my feet.

"Odd," I said. "Did I do that myself in a flash of absent-mindedness?"

I walked back, relit one, and as I did so I saw the candle in the right sconce of one of the mirrors wink and go right out, and almost immediately its companion followed it. The flames vanished as if the wick had been suddenly nipped between a finger and thumb, leaving the wick neither glowing nor smoking, but black. While I stood gaping the candle at the foot of the bed went out, and the shadows seemed to take another step toward me.

"This won't do!" said I, and first one and then another candle on the mantelshelf followed.

"What's up?" I cried, with a queer high note getting into my voice somehow. At that the candle on the corner of the wardrobe went out, and the one I had relit in the alcove followed.

"Steady on!" I said, "those candles are wanted," speaking with a half-hysterical facetiousness, and scratching away at a match the while, "for the mantel candlesticks." My hands trembled so much that twice I missed the rough paper of the matchbox. As the mantel emerged from darkness again, two candles in the remoter end of the room were eclipsed. But with the same match I also relit the larger mirror candles, and those on the floor near the doorway, so that for the moment I seemed to gain on the extinctions. But then in a noiseless volley there vanished four lights at once in different corners of the room, and I struck another match in quivering haste, and stood hesitating whither to take it.

As I stood undecided, an invisible hand seemed to sweep out the two candles on the table. With a cry of terror I dashed at the alcove, then into the corner and then into the window, relighting three as two more vanished by the fireplace, and then, perceiving a better way, I dropped matches on the iron-bound deedbox in the corner, and caught up the bedroom candlestick. With this I avoided the delay of striking matches, but for all that the steady process of extinction went on, and the shadows I feared and fought against returned, and crept in upon me, first a step gained on this side of me, then on that. I was now almost frantic with the horror of the coming darkness, and my self-possession deserted me. I leaped panting from candle to candle in a vain struggle against that remorseless advance.

I bruised myself in the thigh against the table, I sent a chair headlong, I stumbled and fell and whisked the cloth from the table in my fall. My candle rolled away from me and I snatched another as I rose. Abruptly this was blown out as I swung it off the table by the wind of my sudden movement, and immediately the two remaining candles followed. But there was light still in the room, a red light, that streamed across the ceiling and staved off the shadows from me. The fire! Of course I could still thrust my candle between the bars and relight it.

I turned to where the flames were still dancing between the glowing coals and splashing red reflections upon the furniture; made two steps toward the grate, and incontinently the flames dwindled and vanished, the glow vanished, the reflections rushed together and disappeared, and as I thrust the candle between the bars darkness closed upon me like the shutting of an eye, wrapped about me in a stifling embrace, sealed my vision, and crushed the last vestiges of self-possession from my brain. And it was not only palpable darkness, but intolerable terror. The candle fell from my hands. I flung out my arms in a vain effort to thrust that ponderous blackness away from me, and lifting up my voice, screamed with all my might, once, twice, thrice. Then I think I must have staggered to my feet. I know I thought suddenly of the moonlit corridor, and with my head bowed and my arms over my face, made a stumbling run for the door.

But I had forgotten the exact position of the door, and I struck myself heavily against the corner of the bed. I staggered back, turned, and was either struck or struck myself against some other bulky furnishing. I have a vague memory of battering myself thus to and fro in the darkness, of a heavy blow at last upon my forehead, of a horrible sensation of falling that lasted an age, of my last frantic effort to keep my footing, and then I remember no more.

I opened my eyes in daylight. My head was roughly bandaged, and the man with the withered hand was watching my face. I looked about me trying to remember what had happened, and for a space I could not recollect. I rolled my eyes into the corner and saw the old woman, no longer abstracted, no longer terrible, pouring out some drops of medicine from a little blue phial into a glass. "Where am I?" I said. "I seem to remember you, and yet I can not remember who you are."

They told me then, and I heard of the haunted Red Room as one who hears a tale. "We found you at dawn," said he, "and there was blood on your forehead and lips."

I wondered that I had ever disliked him. The three of them in the daylight seemed commonplace old folk enough. The man with the green shade had his head bent as one who sleeps.

It was very slowly I recovered the memory of my experience. "You believe now," said the old man with the withered hand, "that the room is haunted?" He spoke no longer as one who greets an intruder, but as one who condoles with a friend.

"Yes," said I, "the room is haunted."

"And you have seen it. And we who have been here all our lives have never set eyes upon it. Because we have never dared. Tell us, is it truly the old earl who—"

"No," said I, "it is not."

"I told you so"; said the old lady, with the glass in her hand. "It is his poor young countess who was frightened—"

"It is not," I said. "There is neither ghost of earl nor ghost of countess in that room; there is no ghost there at all, but worse, far worse, something impalpable—"

"Well?" they said.

"The worst of all the things that haunt poor mortal men," said I; "and that is, in all its nakedness—'Fear!' Fear that will not have light nor sound, that will not bear with reason, that deafens and darkens and overwhelms. It followed me through the corridor, it fought against me in the room—"

I stopped abruptly. There was an interval of silence. My hand went up to my bandages. "The candles went out one after another, and I fled—"

Then the man with the shade lifted his face sideways to see me and spoke.

"That is it," said he. "I knew that was it. A Power of Darkness. To put such a curse upon a home! It lurks there always. You can feel it even in the day-time, even of a bright summer's day, in the hangings, in the curtains, keeping behind you however you face about. In the dusk it creeps in the corridor and follows you, so that you dare not turn. It is even as you say. Fear itself in that room. Black Fear . . . And there it will be . . . so long as this house of sin endures."

THE LEGEND OF SLEEPY HOLLOW

By WASHINGTON IRVING

(Found among the papers of the late Diedrich Knickerbocker.)

> "A pleasing land of drowsy head it was,
> Of dreams that wave before the half-shut eye;
> And of gay castles in the clouds that pass,
> Forever flushing round a summer sky."
> —*Castle of Indolence.*

In the bosom of one of those spacious coves which indent the eastern shore of the Hudson, at that broad expansion of the river denominated by the ancient Dutch navigators the Tappaan Zee, and where they always prudently shortened sail and implored the protection of St. Nicholas when they crossed, there lies a small market town or rural port, which by some is called Greensburgh, but which is more generally and properly known by the name of Tarry Town.

This name was given it, we are told, in former days, by the good housewives of the adjacent country, from the inveterate propensity of their husbands to linger about the village tavern on market days. Be that as it may, I do not vouch for the fact, but merely advert to it, for the sake of being precise and authentic. Not far from this village, perhaps about three miles, there is a little valley or rather lap of land among high hills, which is one of the quietest places in the whole world. A small brook glides through it, with just murmur enough to lull one to repose, and the occasional whistle of a quail, or tapping of a woodpecker, is almost the only sound that ever breaks in upon the uniform tranquillity.

I recollect that, when a stripling, my first exploit in squirrel-shooting was in a grove of tall walnut-trees that shades one side of the valley. I had wandered into it at noon-time, when all nature is peculiarly quiet, and was startled by the roar of my own gun, as it broke the sabbath stillness around and was prolonged and reverberated by the angry echoes. If ever I should wish for a retreat whither I might steal from the world and its distractions, and dream quietly away the remnant of a troubled life, I know of none more promising than this little valley.

From the listless repose of the place and the peculiar character of its inhabitants, who are descendants from the original Dutch settlers, this sequestered glen has long been known by the name of Sleepy Hollow, and its rustic lads are called the Sleepy Hollow Boys throughout all the neighboring country. A drowsy, dreamy influence seems to hang over the land and to pervade the very atmosphere. Some say that the place was bewitched by a high German doctor, during the early days of the settlement; others, that an old Indian chief, the prophet or wizard of his tribe, held his powwows there before the country was discovered by Master Hendrick Hudson. Certain it is, the place still continues under the sway of some witching power that holds a spell over the minds of the good people, causing them to walk in a continual reverie. They are given to all kinds of marvelous beliefs; are subject to trances and visions, and frequently see strange sights, and hear music and voices in the air.

The whole neighborhood abounds with local tales, haunted spots, and twilight superstitions; stars shoot and meteors glare oftener across the valley than in any other part of the country, and the nightmare, with her whole nine fold, seems to make it the favorite scene of her gambols.

The dominant spirit, however, that haunts this enchanted region and seems to be commander-in-chief of all the powers of the air, the apparition of a figure on horseback without a head. It is said by some to be the ghost of a Hessian trooper, whose head had been carried away by a cannon-ball in some nameless battle during the revolutionary war, and who is ever and anon seen by the country folk, hurrying along in the gloom of night, as if on the wings of the wind. His haunts are not confined to the valley, but extend at times to the adjacent roads, and especially to the vicinity of a church that is at no great distance. Indeed, certain of the most authentic historians of those parts, who have been careful in collecting and collating the floating facts concerning this specter, allege that, the body of the trooper having been buried in the churchyard, the ghost rides forth to the scene of battle in mighty quest of his head, and that the rushing speed with which he sometimes passes along the hollow like a midnight blast is owing to his being belated and in a hurry to get back to the churchyard before daybreak.

Such is the general purport of this legendary superstition, which has furnished materials for many a wild story in that region of shadows, and the specter is known at all the country firesides by the name of The Headless Horseman of Sleepy Hollow.

It is remarkable that the visionary propensity I have mentioned is not confined to the native inhabitants of the valley, but is unconsciously imbibed by every one who resides there for a time. However wide awake they may have been before they entered that sleepy region, they are sure, in a little time, to inhale the witching influence of the air, and begin to grow imaginative—to dream dreams and see apparitions.

I mention this peaceful spot with all possible laud; for it is in such little retired Dutch valleys, found here and there embosomed in the great State of New York, that population, manners and customs remain fixed, while the great torrent of migration and improvement, which is making such incessant changes in other parts of this restless country, sweeps by them unobserved. They are like those little nooks of still water which border a rapid stream, where we may see the straw and bubble riding quietly at anchor, or slowly revolving in their mimic harbor, undisturbed by the rush of the passing current. Tho many years have elapsed since I trod the drowsy shades of Sleepy Hollow, yet I question whether I should not still find the same trees and the same families vegetating in its sheltered bosom.

In this by-place of nature there abode, in a remote period of American history, that is to say, some thirty years since, a worthy wight of the name of Ichabod Crane, who sojourned, or, as he expressed it, "tarried," in Sleepy Hollow, for the purpose of instructing the children of the vicinity. He was a native of Connecticut, a State which supplies the Union with pioneers for the mind as well as for the forest, and sends forth yearly its legions of frontier woodmen and country schoolmasters.

The cognomen of Crane was not inapplicable to his person. He was tall, but exceedingly lank, with narrow shoulders, long arms and legs, hands that dangled a mile out of his sleeves, feet that might have served for shovels, and his whole frame most loosely hung together. His head was small and flat at top, with huge ears, large green glassy eyes, and a long snipe nose, so that it looked like a weathercock perched upon his spindle neck to tell which way the wind blew. To see him striding along the profile of a hill on a windy day, with his clothes bagging and fluttering about him, one might have mistaken him for the genius of famine descending upon the earth, or some scarecrow eloped from a cornfield.

His schoolhouse was a low building of one large room, rudely constructed of logs, the windows partly glazed and partly patched with leaves of copy-books. It was most ingeniously secured at vacant hours by a withe twisted in the handle of the door, and stakes set against the window-shutters; so that, tho a thief might get in with perfect ease, he would find some embarrassment in getting out—an idea most probably borrowed by the architect, Yost Van Houten, from the mystery of an eelpot. The schoolhouse stood in a rather lonely but pleasant situation, just at the foot of a woody hill, with a brook running close by and a formidable birch-tree growing at one end of it. From hence the low murmur of his pupils' voices, conning over their lessons, might be heard of a drowsy summer's day, like the hum of a beehive; interrupted now and then by the authoritative voice of the master in the tone of menace or command; or, peradventure, by the appalling sound of the birch, as he urged some tardy loiterer along the flowery path of knowledge. Truth to say, he was a conscientious man, that ever bore in mind the golden maxim, "spare the rod and spoil the child."—Ichabod Crane's scholars certainly were not spoiled.

I would not have it imagined, however, that he was

one of those cruel potentates of the school who joy in
the smart of their subjects; on the contrary, he administered justice with discrimination rather than severity,
taking the burden off the backs of the weak and laying
it on those of the strong. Your mere puny stripling,
that winced at the least flourish of the rod, was passed
by with indulgence; but the claims of justice were
satisfied by inflicting a double portion on some little,
tough, wrong-headed, broad-skirted Dutch urchin, who
sulked and swelled and grew dogged and sullen beneath
the birch. All this he called "doing his duty by their
parents"; and he never inflicted a chastisement without
following it by the assurance, so consolatory to the
smarting urchin, that "he would remember it and thank
him for it the longest day he had to live."

When school hours were over, he was even the companion and playmate of the larger boys; and on holy-
day afternoons would convoy some of the smaller ones
home, who happened to have pretty sisters, or good
housewives for mothers, noted for the comforts of the
cupboard. Indeed, it behooved him to keep on good
terms with his pupils. The revenue arising from his
school was small, and would have been scarcely sufficient to furnish him with daily bread, for he was a
huge feeder, and, tho lank, had the dilating powers
of an anaconda; but to help out his maintenance, he
was, according to country custom in those parts,
boarded and lodged at the houses of the farmers whose
children he instructed. With these he lived successively
a week at a time, thus going the rounds of the neighborhood with all his worldly effects tied up in a cotton
handkerchief.

That all this might not be too onerous on the purses
of his rustic patrons, who are apt to consider the costs of

schooling a grievous burden and schoolmasters as mere
drones, he had various ways of rendering himself both
useful and agreeable. He assisted the farmers occasionally in the lighter labors of their farms; helped to
make hay; mended the fences; took the horses to
water; drove the cows from pasture, and cut wood for
the winter fire. He laid aside, too, all the dominant
dignity and absolute sway with which he lorded it in
his little empire, the school, and became wonderfully
gentle and ingratiating. He found favor in the eyes of
the mothers, by petting the children, particularly the
youngest; and like the lion bold, which whilom so
magnanimously the lamb did hold, he would sit with a
child on one knee and rock a cradle with his foot for
whole hours together.

In addition to his other vocations, he was the singing-master of the neighborhood, and picked up many
bright shillings by instructing the young folks in
psalmody. It was a matter of no little vanity to him
on Sundays to take his station in front of the church
gallery, with a band of chosen singers; where, in his
own mind, he completely carried away the palm from
the parson. Certain it is, his voice resounded far above
all the rest of the congregation, and there are peculiar
quavers still to be heard in that church, and which may
even be heard half a mile off, quite to the opposite side
of the mill-pond, on a still Sunday morning, which are
said to be legitimately descended from the nose of
Ichabod Crane. Thus by divers little makeshifts, in
that ingenious way which is commonly denominated
"by hook and by crook," the worthy pedagog got on
tolerably enough, and was thought, by all who understood nothing of the labor of head-work, to have a
wonderfully easy life of it.

The schoolmaster is generally a man of some importance in the female circle of a rural neighborhood; being considered a kind of idle gentleman-like personage, of vastly superior taste and accomplishments to the rough country swains, and, indeed, inferior in learning only to the parson. His appearance, therefore, is apt to occasion some little stir at the tea-table of a farmhouse and the addition of a supernumerary dish of cakes or sweetmeats, or, peradventure, the parade of a silver teapot. Our man of letters, therefore, was peculiarly happy in the smiles of all the country damsels. How he would figure among them in the churchyard, between services on Sundays! gathering grapes for them from the wild vines that overrun the surrounding trees; reciting for their amusement all the epitaphs on the tombstones, or sauntering, with a whole bevy of them, along the banks of the adjacent mill-pond; while the more bashful country bumpkins hung sheepishly back, envying his superior elegance and address.

From his half itinerant life, also, he was a kind of traveling gazette, carrying the whole budget of local gossip from house to house, so that his appearance was always greeted with satisfaction. He was, moreover, esteemed by the women as a man of great erudition, for he had read several books quite through, and was a perfect master of Cotton Mather's "History of New England Witchcraft," in which, by the way, he most firmly and potently believed.

He was, in fact, an odd mixture of small shrewdness and simple credulity. His appetite for the marvelous, and his powers of digesting it, were equally extraordinary; and both had been increased by his residence in this spell-bound region. No tale was too gross or monstrous for his capacious swallow. It was often his delight, after his school was dismissed in the afternoon, to stretch himself on the rich bed of clover, bordering the little brook that whimpered by his schoolhouse, and there con over old Mather's direful tales, until the gathering dusk of evening made the printed page a mere mist before his eyes. Then, as he wended his way, by swamp and stream and awful woodland, to the farmhouse where he happened to be quartered, every sound of nature, at that witching hour, fluttered his excited imagination: the moan of the whip-poor-will* from the hillside; the boding cry of the tree-toad, that harbinger of storm; the dreary hooting of the screech-owl, or the sudden rustling in the thicket of birds frightened from their roost. The fireflies, too, which sparkled most vividly in the darkest places, now and then startled him, as one of uncommon brightness would stream across his path; and if, by chance, a huge blockhead of a beetle came winging his blundering flight against him, the poor varlet was ready to give up the ghost, with the idea that he was struck with a witch's token. His only resource on such occasions, either to drown thought or drive away evil spirits, was to sing psalm tunes; and the good people of Sleepy Hollow, as they sat by their doors of an evening, were often filled with awe at hearing his nasal melody, "in linked sweetness long drawn out," floating from the distant hill, or along the dusky road.

Another of his sources of fearful pleasure was to pass long winter evenings with the old Dutch wives, as they sat spinning by the fire, with a row of apples roasting and sputtering along the hearth, and listen to their marvelous tales of ghosts and goblins, and haunted

---

* The whip-poor-will is a bird which is only heard at night. It receives its name from its note, which is thought to resemble those words.

fields and haunted brooks, and haunted bridges and
haunted houses, and particularly of the headless horseman, or galloping Hessian of the Hollow, as they sometimes called him. He would delight them equally by
his anecdotes of witchcraft, and of the direful omens
and portentous sights and sounds in the air, which
prevailed in the earlier times of Connecticut; and would
frighten them wofully with speculations upon comets
and shooting stars, and with the alarming fact that the
world did absolutely turn round, and that they were
half the time topsy-turvy!

But if there was a pleasure in all this, while snugly
cuddling in the chimney corner of a chamber that was
all of a ruddy glow from the crackling wood fire, and
where, of course, no specter dared to show its face, it
was dearly purchased by the terrors of his subsequent
walk homeward. What fearful shapes and shadows
beset his path, amid the dim and ghastly glare of a
snowy night!—With what wistful look did he eye every
trembling ray of light streaming across the waste fields
from some distant window!—How often was he appalled by some shrub covered with snow, which, like a
sheeted specter, beset his very path!—How often did
he shrink with curdling awe at the sound of his own
steps on the frosty crust beneath his feet, and dread to
look over his shoulder, lest he should behold some
uncouth being tramping close behind him!—and how
often was he thrown into complete dismay by some
rushing blast, howling among the trees, in the idea that
it was the galloping Hessian on one of his mighty
scourings!

All these, however, were mere terrors of the night,
fantoms of the mind, that walk in darkness: and tho
he had seen many specters in his time, and had been

more than once beset by Satan in divers shapes in his
lonely perambulations, yet daylight put an end to all
these evils; and he would have passed a pleasant life
of it, in despite of the Devil and all his works, if his
path had not been crossed by a being that causes more
perplexity to mortal man than ghosts, goblins, and the
whole race of witches put together; and that was—a
woman.

Among the musical disciples who assembled, one
evening in each week, to receive his instructions in
psalmody, was Katrina Van Tassel, the daughter and
only child of a substantial Dutch farmer. She was a
blooming lass of fresh eighteen; plump as a partridge,
ripe and melting and rosy-cheeked as one of her father's
peaches, and universally famed, not merely for her
beauty, but her vast expectations. She was withal a
little of a coquet as might be perceived even in her
dress, which was a mixture of ancient and modern
fashions, as most suited to set off her charms. She
wore the ornaments of pure yellow gold which her
great-great-grandmother had brought over from Saar-
dam; the tempting stomacher of the olden time, and
withal a provokingly short petticoat, to display the
prettiest foot and ankle in the country round.

Ichabod Crane had a soft and foolish heart toward
the sex; and it is not to be wondered at that so tempting a morsel soon found favor in his eyes, more
especially after he had visited her in her paternal
mansion. Old Baltus Van Tassel was a perfect picture
of a thriving, contented, liberal-hearted farmer. He
seldom, it is true, sent either his eyes or his thoughts
beyond the boundaries of his own farm; but within
these, everything was snug, happy, and well-condi-
tioned. He was satisfied with his wealth, but not proud

of it; and piqued himself upon the hearty abundance, rather than the style in which he lived. His stronghold was situated on the banks of the Hudson, in one of those green, sheltered, fertile nooks in which the Dutch farmers are so fond of nestling. A great elm-tree spread its broad branches over it, at the foot of which bubbled up a spring of the softest and sweetest water, in a little well formed of a barrel, and then stole sparkling away through the grass, to a neighboring brook that babbled along among alders and dwarf willows. Hard by the farmhouse was a vast barn that might have served for a church, every window and crevice of which seemed bursting forth with the treasures of the farm; the flail was busily resounding within it from morning to night; swallows and martins skimmed twittering about the eaves; and rows of pigeons, some with one eye turned up, as if watching the weather, some with their heads under their wings, or buried in their bosoms, and others, swelling, and cooing, and bowing about their dames, were enjoying the sunshine on the roof. Sleek, unwieldy porkers were grunting in the repose and abundance of their pens, from whence sallied forth, now and then, troops of sucking pigs, as if to snuff the air. A stately squadron of snowy geese were riding in an adjoining pond, convoying whole fleets of ducks; regiments of turkeys were gobbling through the farmyard, and guinea-fowls fretting about it like ill-tempered housewives, with their peevish, discontented cry. Before the barn door strutted the gallant cock, that pattern of a husband, a warrior and a fine gentleman, clapping his burnished wings and crowing in the pride and gladness of his heart —sometimes tearing up the earth with his feet, and then generously calling his ever-hungry family of wives and children to enjoy the rich morsel which he had discovered.

The pedagog's mouth watered as he looked upon this sumptuous promise of luxurious winter fare. In his devouring mind's eye, he pictured to himself every roasting pig running about, with a pudding in its belly and an apple in its mouth; the pigeons were snugly put to bed in a comfortable pie and tucked in with a coverlet of crust; the geese were swimming in their own gravy, and the ducks pairing cosily in dishes, like snug married couples, with a decent competency of onion sauce. In the porkers he saw carved out the future sleek side of bacon and juicy relishing ham; not a turkey, but he beheld daintily trussed up, with its gizzard under its wing, and, peradventure, a necklace of savory sausages; and even bright chanticleer himself lay sprawling on his back, in a side dish, with uplifted claws, as if craving that quarter which his chivalrous spirit disdained to ask while living.

As the enraptured Ichabod fancied all this, and as he rolled his great green eyes over the fat meadow lands, the rich fields of wheat, of rye, of buckwheat and Indian corn, and the orchards burdened with ruddy fruit, which surrounded the warm tenement of Van Tassel, his heart yearned after the damsel who was to inherit these domains, and his imagination expanded with the idea how they might be readily turned into cash, and the money invested in immense tracts of wild land and shingle palaces in the wilderness. Nay, his busy fancy already realized his hopes, and presented to him the blooming Katrina, with a whole family of children, mounted on the top of a wagon loaded with household trumpery, with pots and kettles dangling beneath; and he beheld himself bestriding a pacing mare, with a colt at her heels, setting out for Kentucky, Tennessee—or the Lord knows where!

When he entered the house, the conquest of his heart was complete. It was one of those spacious farmhouses, with high-ridged, but lowly-sloping roofs, built in the style handed down from the first Dutch settlers. The low projecting eaves forming a piazza along the front capable of being closed up in bad weather. Under this were hung flails, harness, various utensils of husbandry, and nets for fishing in the neighboring river. Benches were built along the sides for summer use; and a great spinning-wheel at one end and a churn at the other showed the various uses to which this important porch might be devoted. From this piazza the wonderful Ichabod entered the hall, which formed the center of the mansion, and the place of usual residence. Here, rows of resplendent pewter, ranged on a long dresser, dazzled his eyes. In one corner stood a huge bag of wool, ready to be spun; in another, a quantity of linsey-woolsey just from the loom; ears of Indian corn and strings of dried applies and peaches hung in gay festoons along the walls, mingled with the gaud of red peppers; and a door left ajar gave him a peep into the best parlor, where the claw-footed chairs, and dark mahogany tables, shone like mirrors; andirons, with their accompanying shovel and tongs, glistened from their covert of asparagus tops; mock-oranges and conch shells decorated the mantelpiece; strings of various colored birds' eggs were suspended above it; a great ostrich egg was hung from the center of the room, and a corner cupboard, knowingly left open, displayed immense treasures of old silver and well-mended china.

From the moment Ichabod laid his eyes upon these regions of delight, the peace of his mind was at an end, and his only study was how to gain the affections of the peerless daughter of Van Tassel. In this enterprise, however, he had more real difficulties than generally fell to the lot of a knight-errant of yore, who seldom had anything but giants, enchanters, fiery dragons, and such like easily conquered adversaries, to contend with; and had to make his way merely through gates of iron and brass and walls of adamant to the castle-keep, where the lady of his heart was confined; all which he achieved as easily as a man would carve his way to the center of a Christmas pie, and then the lady gave him her hand as a matter of course. Ichabod, on the contrary, had to win his way to the heart of a country coquet, beset with a labyrinth of whims and caprices, which were forever presenting new difficulties and impediments, and he had to encounter a host of fearful adversaries of real flesh and blood, the numerous rustic admirers who beset every portal to her heart; keeping a watchful and angry eye upon each other, but ready to fly out in the common cause against any new competitor.

Among these, the most formidable was a burly, roaring, roisterous blade, of the name of Abraham, or, according to the Dutch abbreviation, Brom Van Brunt, the hero of the country round, which rung with his feats of strength and hardihood. He was broad-shouldered and double-jointed, with short curly black hair, and a bluff, but not unpleasant countenance, having a mingled air of fun and arrogance. From his Herculean frame and great powers of limb, he had received the nickname of Brom Bones, by which he was universally known. He was famed for great knowledge and skill in horsemanship, being as dexterous on horseback as a Tartar. He was foremost at all races and cock-fights, and with the ascendency which bodily strength always acquires in rustic life, was the umpire in all disputes, setting his hat on one side, and giving his decisions with an air and tone that admitted of no gainsay or appeal. He was always ready for either a fight or a frolic; had more mischief than ill-will in his composition; and, with all his overbearing roughness, there was a strong dash of waggish good-humor at bottom. He had three or four boon companions of his own stamp, who regarded him as their model, and at the head of whom he scoured the country, attending every scene of feud or merriment for miles round. In cold weather, he was distinguished by a fur cap, surmounted with a flaunting fox's tail; and when the folks at a country gathering descried this well-known crest at a distance, whisking about among a squad of hard riders, they always stood by for a squall. Sometimes his crew would be heard dashing along past the farmhouses at midnight, with whoop and halloo, like a troop of Don Cossacks, and the old dames, startled out of their sleep, would listen for a moment till the hurry-scurry had clattered by, and then exclaim, "Ay, there goes Brom Bones and his gang!" The neighbors looked upon him with a mixture of awe, admiration, and good-will; and when any madcap prank or rustic brawl occurred in the vicinity, always shook their heads, and warranted Brom Bones was at the bottom of it.

This rantipole hero had for some time singled out the blooming Katrina for the object of his uncouth gallantries, and tho his amorous toyings were something like the gentle caresses and endearments of a bear, yet it was whispered that she did not altogether discourage his hopes. Certain it is, his advances were signals for rival candidates to retire, who felt no incli-

nation to cross a lion in his amors; insomuch that
when his horse was seen tied to Van Tassel's paling, on
a Sunday night, a sure sign that his master was court-
ing, or, as it is termed, "sparking," within, all other
suitors passed by in despair and carried the war into
other quarters.

Such was the formidable rival with whom Ichabod
Crane had to contend, and considering all things, a
stouter man than he would have shrunk from the
competition, and a wiser man would have despaired.
He had, however, a happy mixture of pliability and
perseverance in his nature; he was in form and spirit
like a supple-jack—yielding, but tough; tho he bent,
he never broke; and tho he bowed beneath the slightest
pressure, yet, the moment it was away—jerk!—he was
as erect and carried his head as high as ever.

To have taken the field openly against his rival would
have been madness; for he was not a man to be
thwarted in his amors, any more than that stormy
lover, Achilles. Ichabod, therefore, made his advances
in a quiet and gently insinuating manner. Under cover
of his character of singing-master, he made frequent
visits at the farmhouse; not that he had anything to
apprehend from the meddlesome interference of parents,
which is so often a stumbling-block in the path of
lovers. Balt Van Tassel was an easy, indulgent soul;
he loved his daughter better even than his pipe, and
like a reasonable man, and an excellent father, let her
have her way in everything. His notable little wife,
too, had enough to do to attend to her housekeeping
and manage the poultry; for, as she sagely observed,
ducks and geese are foolish things, and must be looked
after, but girls can take care of themselves. Thus,
while the busy dame bustled about the house, or plied

her spinning-wheel at one end of the piazza, honest
Balt would sit smoking his evening pipe at the other,
watching the achievements of a little wooden warrior,
who, armed with a sword in each hand, was most
valiantly fighting the wind on the pinnacle of the barn.
In the meantime, Ichabod would carry on his suit with
the daughter by the side of the spring under the great
elm, or sauntering along in the twilight, that hour so
favorable to the lover's eloquence.

I profess not to know how women's hearts are wooed
and won. To me they have always been matters of
riddle and admiration. Some seem to have but one
vulnerable point, or door of access; while others have
a thousand avenues, and may be captured in a thousand
different ways. It is a great triumph of skill to gain
the former, but a still greater proof of generalship to
maintain possession of the latter, for a man must battle
for his fortress at every door and window. He that
wins a thousand common hearts is therefore entitled to
some renown; but he who keeps undisputed sway over
the heart of a coquet, is indeed a hero. Certain it is,
this was not the case with the redoubtable Brom Bones;
and from the moment Ichabod Crane made his advances, the interests of the former evidently declined:
his horse was no longer seen tied at the palings on
Sunday nights, and a deadly feud gradually arose between him and the preceptor of Sleepy Hollow.

Brom, who had a degree of rough chivalry in his
nature, would fain have carried matters to open war-
fare, and settled their pretensions to the lady according
to the mode of those most concise and simple reasoners,
the knights-errant of yore—by single combat; but
Ichabod was too conscious of the superior might of his
adversary to enter the lists against him; he had over-

heard the boast of Bones, that he would "double the schoolmaster up, and put him on a shelf"; and he was too wary to give him an opportunity. There was something extremely provoking in this obstinately pacific system; it left Brom no alternative but to draw upon the funds of rustic waggery in his disposition, and to play off boorish practical jokes upon his rival. Ichabod became the object of whimsical persecution to Bones and his gang of rough riders. They harried his hitherto peaceful domains; smoked out his singing-school, by stopping up the chimney; broke into the schoolhouse at night, in spite of its formidable fastenings of withe and window stakes, and turned everything topsy-turvy; so that the poor schoolmaster began to think all the witches in the country held their meetings there. But what was still more annoying, Brom took all opportunities of turning him into ridicule in presence of his mistress, and had a scoundrel dog whom he taught to whine in the most ludicrous manner, and introduced as a rival of Ichabod's, to instruct her in psalmody.

In this way, matters went on for some time, without producing any material effect on the relative situations of the contending powers. On a fine autumnal afternoon, Ichabod, in pensive mood, sat enthroned on the lofty stool from whence he usually watched all the concerns of his little literary realm. In his hand he swayed a ferule, that scepter of despotic power; the birch of justice reposed on three nails, behind the throne, a constant terror to evil doers; while on the desk before him might be seen sundry contraband articles and prohibited weapons, detected upon the persons of idle urchins, such as half-munched apples, popguns, whirligigs, fly-cages, and whole legions of rampant little paper game-cocks. Apparently there had been

some appalling act of justice recently inflicted, for his
scholars were all busily intent upon their books, or
slyly whispering behind them with one eye kept upon
the master; and a kind of buzzing stillness reigned
throughout the schoolroom. It was suddenly interrupted by the appearance of a negro in towcloth jacket
and trousers, a round crowned fragment of a hat, like
the cap of Mercury, and mounted on the back of a
ragged, wild, half-broken colt, which he managed with
a rope by way of halter. He came clattering up to
the school door with an invitation to Ichabod to attend
a merry-making, or "quilting frolic," to be held that
evening at Mynheer Van Tassel's; and having delivered
his message with that air of importance, and effort at
fine language, which a negro is apt to display on petty
embassies of the kind, he dashed over the brook, and
was seen scampering away up the hollow, full of the
importance and hurry of his mission.

All was now bustle and hubbub in the late quiet
schoolroom. The scholars were hurried through their
lessons, without stopping at trifles; those who were
nimble skipped over half with impunity, and those who
were tardy had a smart application now and then in the
rear, to quicken their speed, or help them over a tall
word. Books were flung aside, without being put away
on the shelves; inkstands were overturned, benches
thrown down, and the whole school was turned loose
an hour before the usual time; bursting forth like a
legion of young imps, yelping and racketing about the
green, in joy at their early emancipation.

The gallant Ichabod now spent at least an extra
half-hour at his toilet, brushing and furbishing up his
best, and indeed only suit of rusty black, and arranging
his looks by a bit of broken looking-glass that hung up

in the schoolhouse. That he might make his appearance before his mistress in the true style of a cavalier, he borrowed a horse from the farmer with whom he was domiciliated, a choleric old Dutchman, of the name of Hans Van Ripper, and thus gallantly mounted, issued forth like a knight-errant in quest of adventures. But it is meet I should, in the true spirit of romantic story, give some account of the looks and equipment of my hero and his steed. The animal he bestrode was a broken-down plow-horse that had outlived almost everything but his viciousness. He was gaunt and shagged, with a ewe neck and a head like a hammer; his rusty mane and tail were tangled and knotted with burrs; one eye had lost its pupil, and was glaring and spectral, but the other had the gleam of a genuine devil in it. Still he must have had fire and mettle in his day, if we may judge from his name, which was Gunpowder. He had, in fact, been a favorite steed of his master's, the choleric Van Ripper, who was a furious rider, and had infused, very probably, some of his own spirit into the animal; for, old and broken-down as he looked, there was more of the lurking devil in him than in any young filly in the country.

Ichabod was a suitable figure for such a steed. He rode with short stirrups, which brought his knees nearly up to the pommel of the saddle; his sharp elbows stuck out like grasshoppers'; he carried his whip perpendicularly in his hand, like a scepter, and as the horse jogged on, the motion of his arms was not unlike the flapping of a pair of wings. A small wool hat rested on the top of his nose, for so his scanty strip of forehead might be called, and the skirts of his black coat fluttered out almost to the horse's tail. Such was the appearance of Ichabod and his steed as they shambled out of the gate of Hans Van Ripper, and it was altogether such an apparition as is seldom to be met with in broad daylight.

It was, as I have said, a fine autumnal day; the sky was clear and serene, and nature wore that rich and golden livery which we always associate with the idea of abundance. The forests had put on their sober brown and yellow, while some trees of the tenderer kind had been nipped by the frosts into brilliant dyes of orange, purple, and scarlet. Streaming files of wild ducks began to make their appearance high in the air; the bark of the squirrel might be heard from the groves of beech and hickory-nuts, and the pensive whistle of the quail at intervals from the neighboring stubble-field.

The small birds were taking their farewell banquets. In the fulness of their revelry, they fluttered, chirping and frolicking, from bush to bush and tree to tree, capricious from the very profusion and variety around them. There was the honest cock-robin, the favorite game of stripling sportsmen, with its loud querulous note, and the twittering blackbirds flying in sable clouds; and the golden-winged woodpecker, with his crimson crest, his broad black gorget and splendid plumage; and the cedar-bird, with its red-tipped wings and yellow-tipped tail, and its little monteiro cap of feathers; and the blue jay, that noisy coxcomb, in his gay light blue coat and white underclothes, screaming and chattering, nodding, and bobbing, and bowing, and pretending to be on good terms with every songster of the grove.

As Ichabod jogged slowly on his way, his eye, ever open to every symptom of culinary abundance, ranged with delight over the treasures of jolly autumn. On all sides he beheld vast store of apples, some hanging in oppressive opulence on the trees, some gathered into baskets and barrels for the market, others heaped up in rich piles for the cider-press. Further on he beheld great fields of Indian corn, with its golden ears peeping from their leafy coverts and holding out the promise of cakes and hasty-pudding; and the yellow pumpkins lying beneath them, turning up their fair round bellies to the sun, and giving ample prospects of the most luxurious of pies; and anon he passed the fragrant buckwheat fields, breathing the odor of the beehive, and as he beheld them, soft anticipations stole over his mind of dainty slap-jacks, well-buttered, and garnished with honey or treacle, by the delicate little dimpled hand of Katrina Van Tassel.

Thus feeding his mind with many sweet thoughts and "sugared suppositions," he journeyed along the sides of a range of hills which look out upon some of the goodliest scenes of the mighty Hudson. The sun gradually wheeled his broad disk down into the west. The wide bosom of the Tappaan Zee lay motionless and glassy, excepting that here and there a gentle undulation waved and prolonged the blue shadow of the distant mountain. A few amber clouds floated in the sky, without a breath of air to move them. The horizon was of a fine golden tint, changing gradually into a pure apple green, and from that into the deep blue of the mid-heaven. A slanting ray lingered on the woody crests of the precipices that overhung some parts of the river, giving greater depth to the dark gray and purple of their rocky sides. A sloop was loitering in the distance, dropping slowly down with the tide, her sail hanging uselessly against the mast; and as the reflection of the sky gleamed along the still water, it seemed as if the vessel was suspended in the air.

It was toward evening that Ichabod arrived at the castle of the Heer Van Tassel, which he found thronged with the pride and flower of the adjacent country. Old farmers, a spare leathern-faced race, in homespun coats and breeches, blue stockings, huge shoes, and magnificent pewter buckles. Their brisk, withered little dames, in close crimped caps, long-waisted gowns, homespun petticoats, with scissors and pin-cushions, and gay calico pockets hanging on the outside. Buxom lasses, almost as antiquated as their mothers, except where a straw hat, a fine ribbon, or perhaps a white frock, gave symptoms of city innovations. The sons in short square-skirted coats, with rows of stupendous brass buttons, and their hair generally cued in the fashion of the times, especially if they could procure an eelskin for the purpose, it being esteemed throughout that country as a potent nourisher and strengthener of the hair.

Brom Bones, however, was the hero of the scene, having come to the gathering on his favorite steed Daredevil, a creature, like himself, full of mettle and mischief, and which no one but himself could manage. He was, in fact, noted for preferring vicious animals, given to all kinds of tricks which kept the rider in constant risk of his neck, for he held a tractable well-broken horse as unworthy of a lad of spirit.

Fain would I pause to dwell upon the world of charms that burst upon the enraptured gaze of my hero, as he entered the state parlor of Van Tassel's mansion. Not those of the bevy of buxom lasses, with their luxurious display of red and white, but the ample charms of a genuine Dutch country tea-table, in the sumptuous time of autumn. Such heaped-up platters of cakes of various and almost indescribable kinds, known only to experienced Dutch housewives! There was the doughty doughnut, the tender oly-koek, and the crisp and crumbling cruller; sweet cakes and short cakes, ginger cakes and honey cakes, and the whole family of cakes. And then there were apple pies, and peach pies, and pumpkin pies; besides slices of ham and smoked beef; and moreover delectable dishes of preserved plums, and peaches, and pears, and quinces; not to mention broiled shad and roasted chickens; together with bowls of milk and cream, all mingled higgledy-piggledy, pretty much as I have enumerated them, with the motherly teapot sending up its clouds of vapor from the midst—Heaven bless the mark! I want breath and time to discuss this banquet as it deserves, and am too eager to get on with my story. Happily, Ichabod Crane was not in so great a hurry as his historian, but did ample justice to every dainty.

He was a kind and thankful creature, whose heart dilated in proportion as his skin was filled with good cheer, and whose spirits rose with eating, as some men's do with drink. He could not help, too, rolling his large eyes round him as he ate, and chuckling with the possibility that he might one day be lord of all this scene of almost unimaginable luxury and splendor. Then, he thought, how soon he'd turn his back upon the old schoolhouse; snap his fingers in the face of Hans Van Ripper, and every other niggardly patron, and kick any itinerant pedagog out of doors that should dare to call him comrade!

Old Baltus Van Tassel moved about among his guests with a face dilated with content and good-humor, round and jolly as the harvest moon. His hospitable attentions were brief, but expressive, being confined to a shake of the hand, a slap on the shoulder, a loud laugh, and a pressing invitation to "fall to and help themselves."

And now the sound of the music from the common room, or hall, summoned to the dance. The musician was an old gray-headed negro, who had been the itinerant orchestra of the neighborhood for more than half a century. His instrument was as old and battered as himself. The greater part of the time he scraped away on two or three strings, accompanying every movement of the bow with a motion of the head; bowing almost to the ground, and stamping with his foot whenever a fresh couple were to start.

Ichabod prided himself upon his dancing as much as upon his vocal powers. Not a limb, not a fiber about him was idle; and to have seen his loosely hung frame in full motion, and clattering about the room, you would have thought St. Vitus himself, that blessed patron of the dance, was figuring before you in person. He was the admiration of all the negroes; who, having gathered, of all ages and sizes, from the farm and the neighborhood, stood forming a pyramid of shining black faces at every door and window, gazing with delight at the scene, rolling their white eyeballs, and showing grinning rows of ivory from ear to ear. How could the flogger of urchins be otherwise than animated and joyous?—the lady of his heart was his partner in the dance, and smiling graciously in reply to all his amorous oglings; while Brom Bones, sorely smitten with love and jealousy, sat brooding by himself in one corner.

When the dance was at an end, Ichabod was attracted to a knot of the sager folks, who, with Old Van Tassel, sat smoking at one end of the piazza, gossiping over former times, and drawling out long stories about the war.

This neighborhood, at the time of which I am speaking, was one of those highly favored places which abound with chronicle and great men. The British and American line had run near it during the war; it had, therefore, been the scene of marauding, and infested with refugees, cowboys, and all kind of border chivalry. Just sufficient time had elapsed to enable each storyteller to dress up his tale with a little becoming fiction, and, in the indistinctness of his recollection, to make himself the hero of every exploit.

There was the story of Doffue Martling, a large blue-bearded Dutchman, who had nearly taken a British frigate with an old iron nine-pounder from a mud breastwork, only that his gun burst at the sixth discharge. And there was an old gentleman who shall be nameless, being too rich a mynheer to be lightly mentioned, who, in the battle of White Plains, being an excellent master of defense, parried a musket-ball with a small-sword, insomuch that he absolutely felt it whiz round the blade and glance off at the hilt; in proof of which he was ready at any time to show the sword, with the hilt a little bent. There were several more that had been equally great in the field, not one of whom but was persuaded that he had a considerable hand in bringing the war to a happy termination.

But all these were nothing to the tales of ghosts and apparitions that succeeded. The neighborhood is rich in legendary treasures of the kind. Local tales and superstitions thrive best in these sheltered long-settled retreats; but are trampled under foot by the shifting throng that forms the population of most of our country places. Besides, there is no encouragement for ghosts in most of our villages, for they have scarcely had time to finish their first nap, and turn themselves in their graves, before their surviving friends have traveled away from the neighborhood: so that when they turn out at night to walk their rounds, they have no acquaintance left to call upon. This is perhaps the reason why we so seldom hear of ghosts except in our long-established Dutch communities.

The immediate cause, however, of the prevalence of supernatural stories in these parts was doubtless owing to the vicinity of Sleepy Hollow. There was a contagion in the very air that blew from that haunted region; it breathed forth an atmosphere of dreams and fancies infecting all the land. Several of the Sleepy Hollow people were present at Van Tassel's, and, as usual, were doling out their wild and wonderful legends. Many dismal tales were told about funeral trains, and mourning cries and wailings heard and seen about the great tree where the unfortunate Major André was taken, and which stood in the neighborhood. Some mention was made also of the woman in white, that haunted the dark glen at Raven Rock, and was often heard to shriek on winter nights before a storm, having perished there in the snow. The chief part of the stories, however, turned upon the favorite specter of Sleepy Hollow, the headless horseman, who had been heard several times of late, patroling the country, and, it is said, tethered his horse nightly among the graves in the churchyard.

The sequestered situation of this church seems always to have made it a favorite haunt of troubled spirits. It stands on a knoll, surrounded by locust trees and lofty elms, from among which its decent, whitewashed walls shine modestly forth, like Christian purity, beaming through the shades of retirement. A gentle slope descends from it to a silver sheet of water, bordered by high trees, between which peeps may be caught at the blue hills of the Hudson. To look upon its grass-grown yard, where the sunbeams seem to sleep so quietly, one would think that there at least the dead might rest in peace. On one side of the church extends a wide woody dell, along which raves a large brook among broken rocks and trunks of fallen trees. Over a deep black part of the stream, not far from the church, was formerly thrown a wooden bridge; the road that led to it, and the bridge itself, were thickly shaded by overhanging trees, which cast a gloom about it, even in daytime; but occasioned a fearful darkness at night. Such was one of the favorite haunts of the headless horseman, and the place where he was most frequently encountered. The tale was told of old Brouwer, a most heretical disbeliever in ghosts, how he met the horseman returning from his foray into Sleepy Hollow, and was obliged to get up behind him; how they galloped over bush and brake, over hill and swamp, until they reached the bridge; when the horseman suddenly turned into a skeleton, threw old Brouwer into the brook, and sprang away over the treetops with a clap of thunder.

This story was immediately matched by a thrice marvelous adventure of Brom Bones, who made light of the galloping Hessian as an arrant jockey. He affirmed that, on returning one night from the neighboring village of Sing Sing, he had been overtaken by this midnight trooper; that he had offered to race with him for a bowl of punch, and should have won it too, for Daredevil beat the goblin horse all hollow, but just as they came to the church bridge the Hessian bolted, and vanished in a flash of fire.

All these tales, told in that drowsy undertone with which men talk in the dark, the countenance of the listeners only now and then receiving a casual gleam from the glare of a pipe, sunk deep in the mind of Ichabod. He repaid them in kind with large extracts from his invaluable author, Cotton Mather, and added many marvelous events that had taken place in his native State of Connecticut, and fearful sights which he had seen in his nightly walks about Sleepy Hollow.

The revel now gradually broke up. The old farmers gathered together their families in their wagons, and were heard for some time rattling along the hollow roads, and over the distant hills. Some of the damsels mounted on pillions behind their favorite swains, and their light-hearted laughter, mingled with the clatter of hoofs, echoed along the silent woodlands, sounding fainter and fainter, until they gradually died away—and the late scene of noise and frolic was all silent and deserted. Ichabod only lingered behind, according to the custom of country lovers, to have a tête-à-tête with the heiress, fully convinced that he was now on the high road to success. What passed at this interview I will not pretend to say, for in fact I do not know. Something, however, I fear me, must have gone wrong, for he certainly sallied forth, after no very great interval, with an air quite desolate and chapfallen.—Oh, these women! these women! Could that girl have been playing off any of her coquettish tricks?—Was her encouragement of the poor pedagog all a mere sham to secure her conquest of his rival?—Heaven only knows, not I!—Let it suffice to say, Ichabod stole forth with the air of one who had been sacking a hen-roost, rather

than a fair lady's heart. Without looking to the right
or left to notice the scene of rural wealth on which he
had so often gloated, he went straight to the stable, and
with several hearty cuffs and kicks roused his steed
most uncourteously from the comfortable quarters in
which he was soundly sleeping, dreaming of mountains
of corn and oats, and whole valleys of timothy and
clover.

It was the very witching time of night that Ichabod,
heavy-hearted and crestfallen, pursued his travel homeward, along the sides of the lofty hills which rise above
Tarry Town, and which he had traversed so cheerily in
the afternoon. The hour was as dismal as himself.
Far below him the Tappaan Zee spread its dusky and
indistinct waste of waters, with here and there the tall
mast of a sloop, riding quietly at anchor under the
land. In the dead hush of midnight he could even hear
the barking of the watch-dog from the opposite shore
of the Hudson; but it was so vague and faint as only
to give an idea of his distance from this faithful companion of man. Now and then, too, the long-drawn
crowing of a cock, accidentally awakened, would sound
far, far off, from some farmhouse away among the hills
—but it was like a dreaming sound in his ear. No
signs of life occurred near him, but occasionally the
melancholy chirp of a cricket, or perhaps the guttural
twang of a bullfrog from a neighboring marsh, as if
sleeping uncomfortably, and turning suddenly in his
bed.

All the stories of ghosts and goblins that he had
heard in the afternoon now came crowding upon his
recollection. The night grew darker and darker, the
stars seemed to sink deeper in the sky, and driving
clouds occasionally hid them from his sight. He had

never felt so lonely and dismal. He was, moreover, approaching the very place where many of the scenes of the ghost stories had been laid. In the center of the road stood an enormous tulip tree, which towered like a giant above all the other trees of the neighborhood, and formed a kind of landmark. Its limbs were gnarled and fantastic, large enough to form trunks for ordinary trees, twisting down almost to the earth, and rising again into the air. It was connected with the tragical story of the unfortunate André, who had been taken prisoner hard by; and was universally known by the name of Major André's tree. The common people regarded it with a mixture of respect and superstition, partly out of sympathy for the fate of its ill-starred namesake, and partly from the tales of strange sights and doleful lamentations told concerning it.

As Ichabod approached this fearful tree he began to whistle; he thought his whistle was answered: it was but a blast sweeping sharply through the dry branches. As he approached a little nearer, he thought he saw something white hanging in the midst of the tree: he paused, and ceased whistling; but, on looking more narrowly, perceived that it was a place where the tree had been scathed by lightning and the white wood laid bare. Suddenly he heard a groan—his teeth chattered, and his knees smote against the saddle: it was but the rubbing of one huge bough upon another, as they were swayed about by the breeze. He passed the tree in safety, but new perils lay before him.

About two hundred yards from the tree a small brook crossed the road, and ran into a marshy and thickly wooded glen known by the name of Wiley's Swamp. A few rough logs, laid side by side, served for a bridge over this stream. On that side of the road where the brook entered the wood a group of oaks and chestnuts, matted thick with wild grape-vines, threw a cavernous gloom over it. To pass this bridge was the severest trial. It was at this identical spot that the unfortunate André was captured, and under the covert of those chestnuts and vines were the sturdy yeomen concealed who surprised him. This has ever since been considered a haunted stream, and fearful are the feelings of a schoolboy who has to pass it alone after dark.

As he approached the stream his heart began to thump; he summoned up, however, all his resolution, gave his horse half a score of kicks in the ribs, and attempted to dash briskly across the bridge; but instead of starting forward, the perverse old animal made a lateral movement, and ran broadside against the fence. Ichabod, whose fears increased with the delay, jerked the reins on the other side, and kicked lustily with the contrary foot. It was all in vain; his steed started, it is true, but it was only to plunge to the opposite side of the road into a thicket of brambles and alder bushes. The schoolmaster now bestowed both whip and heel upon the starveling ribs of old Gunpowder, who dashed forward, snuffling and snorting, but came to a stand just by the bridge with a suddenness that had nearly sent his rider sprawling over his head. Just at this moment a plashy tramp by the side of the bridge caught the sensitive ear of Ichabod. In the dark shadow of the grove, on the margin of the brook, he beheld something huge, misshapen, black and towering. It stirred not, but seemed gathering up in the gloom, like some gigantic monster ready to spring upon the traveler.

The hair of the affrighted pedagog rose upon his head with terror. What was to be done? To turn and fly was now too late; and besides, what chance was there of escaping ghost or goblin, if such it was, which could ride upon the wings of the wind? Summoning up, therefore, a show of courage, he demanded in stammering accents—"Who are you?" He received no reply. He repeated his demand in a still more agitated voice. Still there was no answer. Once more he cudgeled the sides of the inflexible Gunpowder, and shutting his eyes, broke forth with involuntary fervor into a psalm tune. Just then the shadowy object of alarm put itself in motion, and with a scramble and a bound stood at once in the middle of the road. Tho the night was dark and dismal, yet the form of the unknown might now in some degree be ascertained. He appeared to be a horseman of large dimensions, and mounted on a black horse of powerful frame. He made no offer of molestation or sociability, but kept aloof on one side of the road, jogging along on the blind side of old Gunpowder, who had now got over his fright and waywardness.

Ichabod, who had no relish for this strange midnight companion, and bethought himself of the adventure of Brom Bones with the galloping Hessian, now quickened his steed, in hopes of leaving him behind. The stranger, however, quickened his horse to an equal pace. Ichabod pulled up, and fell into a walk, thinking to lag behind—the other did the same. His heart began to sink within him; he endeavored to resume his psalm tune, but his parched tongue clove to the roof of his mouth, and he could not utter a stave. There was something in the moody and dogged silence of this pertinacious companion that was mysterious and appalling. It was soon fearfully accounted for. On mounting a rising ground, which brought the figure of his fellow-traveler in relief against the sky, gigantic in height, and muffled in a cloak, Ichabod was horror-struck, on perceiving that he was headless! but his horror was still more increased, on observing that the head, which should have rested on his shoulders, was carried before him on the pommel of his saddle! His terror rose to desperation; he rained a shower of kicks and blows upon Gunpowder, hoping, by a sudden movement, to give his companion the slip—but the specter started full jump with him. Away, then, they dashed through thick and thin; stones flying and sparks flashing at every bound. Ichabod's flimsy garments fluttered in the air, as he stretched his long lank body away over his horse's head, in the eagerness of his flight.

They had now reached the road which turns off to Sleepy Hollow; but Gunpowder, who seemed possessed with a demon, instead of keeping up it, made an opposite turn, and plunged headlong downhill to the left. This road leads through a sandy hollow, shaded by trees for about a quarter of a mile, where it crosses the bridge famous in goblin story; and just beyond swells the green knoll on which stands the whitewashed church.

As yet the panic of the steed had given his unskilful rider an apparent advantage in the chase; but just as he had got half-way through the hollow, the girths of the saddle gave way, and he felt it slipping from under him. He seized it by the pommel, and endeavored to hold it firm, but in vain; and had just time to save himself by clasping old Gunpowder round the neck, when the saddle fell to the earth, and he heard it trampled under foot by his pursuer. For a moment the terror of Hans Van Ripper's wrath passed across his mind—for it was his Sunday saddle; but this was no time for petty fears: the goblin was hard on his haunches; and (unskilful rider that he was!) he had much ado to maintain his seat; sometimes slipping on one side, sometimes on another, and sometimes jolted on the high ridge of his horse's backbone, with a violence that he verily feared would cleave him asunder.

An opening in the trees now cheered him with the hopes that the church bridge was at hand. The wavering reflection of a silver star in the bosom of the brook told him that he was not mistaken. He saw the walls of the church dimly glaring under the trees beyond. He recollected the place where Brom Bones's ghostly competitor had disappeared. "If I can but reach that bridge," thought Ichabod, "I am safe." Just then he heard the black steed panting and blowing close behind him; he even fancied that he felt his hot breath. Another convulsive kick in the ribs, and old Gunpowder sprung upon the bridge; he thundered over the resounding planks; he gained the opposite side, and now Ichabod cast a look behind to see if his pursuer should vanish, according to rule, in a flash of fire and brimstone. Just then he saw the goblin rising in his stirrups, and in the very act of hurling his head at him. Ichabod endeavored to dodge the horrible missile, but too late. It encountered his cranium with a tremendous crash—he was tumbled headlong into the dust, and Gunpowder, the black steed, and the goblin rider, passed by like a whirlwind.

The next morning the old horse was found without his saddle, and with the bridle under his feet, soberly cropping the grass at his master's gate. Ichabod did not make his appearance at breakfast—dinner-hour came, but no Ichabod. The boys assembled at the schoolhouse, and strolled idly about the banks of the brook; but no schoolmaster. Hans Van Ripper now began to feel some uneasiness about the fate of poor Ichabod, and his saddle. An inquiry was set on foot, and after diligent investigation they came upon his traces. In one part of the road leading to the church was found the saddle trampled in the dirt; the tracks of horses' hoofs deeply dented in the road, and evidently at furious speed, were traced to the bridge, beyond which, on the bank of a broad part of the brook, where the water ran deep and black, was found the hat of the unfortunate Ichabod, and close beside it a shattered pumpkin.

The brook was searched, but the body of the schoolmaster was not to be discovered. Hans Van Ripper, as executor of his estate, examined the bundle which contained all his worldly effects. They consisted of two shirts and a half; two stocks for the neck; a pair or two of worsted stockings; an old pair of corduroy small-clothes; a rusty razor; a book of psalm tunes full of dog's ears; and a broken pitch-pipe. As to the books and furniture of the schoolhouse, they belonged to the community, excepting Cotton Mather's "History of Witchcraft," a New England Almanac, and a book of dreams and fortune-telling; in which last was a sheet of foolscap much scribbled and blotted, by several fruitless attempts to make a copy of verses in honor of the heiress of Van Tassel. These magic books and the poetic scrawl were forthwith consigned to the flames by Hans Van Ripper; who, from that time forward, determined to send his children no more to school; observing that he never knew any good come of this same reading and writing. Whatever money the schoolmaster possessed, and he had received his quarter's pay but a day or two before, he must have had about his person at the time of his disappearance.

The mysterious event caused much speculation at the church on the following Sunday. Knots of gazers and gossips were collected in the churchyard, at the bridge, and at the spot where the hat and pumpkin had been found. The stories of Brouwer, of Bones, and a whole budget of others, were called to mind; and when they had diligently considered them all, and compared them with the symptoms of the present case, they shook their heads, and came to the conclusion that Ichabod had been carried off by the galloping Hessian. As he was a bachelor, and in nobody's debt, nobody troubled his head any more about him! the school was removed to a different quarter of the Hollow, and another pedagog reigned in his stead.

It is true, an old farmer, who had been down to New York on a visit several years after, and from whom this account of the ghostly adventure was received, brought home the intelligence that Ichabod Crane was still alive; that he had left the neighborhood partly through fear of the goblin and Hans Van Ripper, and partly in mortification at having been suddenly dismissed by the heiress; that he had changed his quarters to a distant part of the country; had kept school and studied law at the same time; had been admitted to the bar; turned politician; electioneered; written for the newspapers; and finally had been made a Justice of the Ten Pound Court. Brom Bones too, who, shortly after his rival's disappearance, conducted the blooming Katrina in triumph to the altar, was observed to look exceedingly knowing whenever the story of Ichabod was related, and always burst into a hearty laugh at the mention of the pumpkin; which led some to suspect that he knew more about the matter than he chose to tell.

The old country wives, however, who are the best judges of these matters, maintain to this day that Ichabod was spirited away by supernatural means; and it is a favorite story often told about the neighborhood round the winter evening fire. The bridge became more than ever the object of superstitious awe; and that may be the reason why the road has been altered of late years, so as to approach the church by the border of the mill-pond. The schoolhouse being deserted, soon fell to decay, and was reported to be haunted by the ghost of the unfortunate pedagog; and the plow-boy, loitering homeward of a still summer evening, has often fancied his voice at a distance, chanting a melancholy psalm tune among the tranquil solitudes of Sleepy Hollow.

POSTSCRIPT

FOUND IN THE HANDWRITING OF MR. KNICKERBOCKER

The preceding Tale is given, almost in the precise words in which I heard it related at a Corporation meeting of the ancient city of the Manhattoes,* at which were present many of its sagest and most illustrious burghers. The narrator was a pleasant, shabby, gentlemanly old fellow in pepper-and-salt clothes, with a sadly humorous face; and one whom I strongly suspected of being poor—he made such efforts to be entertaining. When his story was concluded there was much laughter and approbation, particularly from two or three

---

* New York.

deputy aldermen, who had been asleep the greater part
of the time. There was, however, one tall, dry-looking
old gentleman, with beetling eyebrows, who maintained
a grave and rather severe face throughout; now and
then folding his arms, inclining his head, and looking
down upon the floor, as if turning a doubt over in his
mind. He was one of your wary men, who never laugh
but upon good grounds—when they have reason and
the law on their side. When the mirth of the rest of
the company had subsided, and silence was restored,
he leaned one arm on the elbow of his chair, and stick-
ing the other a-kimbo, demanded, with a slight but
exceedingly sage motion of the head and contraction of
the brow, what was the moral of the story, and what
it went to prove.

The story-teller, who was just putting a glass of
wine to his lips, as a refreshment after his toils, paused
for a moment, looked at his inquirer with an air of
infinite deference, and lowering the glass slowly to the
table, observed that the story was intended most
logically to prove:

"That there is no situation in life but has its advan-
tages and pleasures—provided we will but take a joke
as we find it;

"That, therefore, he that runs races with goblin
troopers is likely to have rough riding of it;

"Ergo, for a country schoolmaster to be refused the
hand of a Dutch heiress is a certain step to high prefer-
ment in the State."

The cautious old gentleman knit his brows tenfold
closer after this explanation, being sorely puzzled by
the ratiocination of the syllogism; while, methought,
the one in the pepper-and-salt eyed him with something
of a triumphant leer. At length he observed, that all

this was very well, but still he thought the story a little on the extravagant—there were one or two points on which he had his doubts:

"Faith, sir," replied the story-teller, "as to that matter, I don't believe one-half of it myself."

D. K.

THE TWO DROVERS

By SIR WALTER SCOTT

Chapter I

It was the day after Doune Fair when my story commences. It had been a brisk market: several dealers had attended from the northern and midland counties in England, and English money had flown so merrily about as to gladden the hearts of the Highland farmers. Many large droves were about to set off for England, under the protection of their owners, or of the topsmen whom they employed in the tedious, laborious, and responsible office of driving the cattle for many hundred miles, from the market where they had been purchased to the fields or farmyards where they were to be fattened for the shambles.

The Highlanders in particular are masters of this difficult trade of driving, which seems to suit them as well as the trade of war. It affords exercise for all their habits of patient endurance and active exertion. They are required to know perfectly the drove-roads, which lie over the wildest tracts of the country, and to avoid as much as possible the highways, which distress the feet of the bullocks, and the turnpikes, which annoy the spirit of the drover; whereas on the broad green or gray track, which leads across the pathless moor, the herd not only move at ease and without taxation, but, if they mind their business, may pick up a mouthful of food by the way. At night, the drovers usually sleep along with their cattle, let the weather be what it will; and many of these hardy men do not once rest under a roof during a journey on foot from Lochaber to Lincolnshire. They are paid very highly, for the trust reposed is of the last importance, as it depends on their prudence, vigilance, and honesty whether the cattle reach the final market in good order, and afford a profit to the grazier. But, as they maintain themselves at their own expense, they are especially economical in that particular. At the period we speak of, a Highland drover was victualled for his long and toilsome journey with a few handfuls of oatmeal and two or three onions, renewed from time to time, and a ram's horn filled with whisky, which he used regularly, but sparingly, every night and morning. His dirk, or skene-dhu (i. e. black knife), so worn as to be concealed beneath the arm, or by the folds of the plaid, was his only weapon, excepting the cudgel with which he directed the movements of the cattle. A Highlander was never so happy as on these occasions. There was a variety in the whole journey which exercised the Celt's natural curiosity and love of motion; there were the constant change of place and scene, the petty adventures incidental to the traffic, and the intercourse with the various farmers, graziers, and traders, intermingled with occasional merry-makings, not the less acceptable to Donald that they were void of expense; and there was the consciousness of superior skill: for the Highlander, a child amongst flocks, is a prince amongst herds, and his natural habits induce him to disdain the shepherd's slothful life, so that he feels himself nowhere more at home than when following a gallant drove of his country cattle in the character of their guardian.

Of the number who left Doune in the morning, and with the purpose we have described, not a glunamie of them all cocked his bonnet more briskly, or gartered his tartan hose under knee over a pair of more promising spigs (legs), than did Robin Oig M'Combich, called familiarly Robin Oig, that is, Young, or the Lesser, Robin. Tho small of stature, as the epithet Oig implies, and not very strongly limbed, he was as light and alert as one of the deer of his mountains. He had an elasticity of step which, in the course of a long march, made many a stout fellow envy him; and the manner in which he busked his plaid and adjusted his bonnet argued a consciousness that so smart a John Highlandman as himself would not pass unnoticed among the Lowland lasses. The ruddy cheek, red lips, and white teeth set off a countenance which had gained by exposure to the weather a healthful and hardy rather than a rugged hue. If Robin Oig did not laugh, or even smile, frequently, as indeed is not the practise among his countrymen, his bright eyes usually gleamed from under his bonnet with an expression of cheerfulness ready to be turned into mirth.

The departure of Robin Oig was an incident in the little town, in and near which he had many friends, male and female. He was a topping person in his way, transacted considerable business on his own behalf, and was entrusted by the best farmers in the Highlands, in preference to any other drover in that district. He might have increased his business to any extent had he condescended to manage it by deputy; but, except a lad or two, sister's sons of his own, Robin rejected the idea of assistance, conscious, perhaps, how much his reputation depended upon his attending in person to the practical discharge of his duty in every instance. He re-

mained, therefore, contented with the highest premium
given to persons of his description, and comforted
himself with the hopes that a few journeys to England
might enable him to conduct business on his own
account in a manner becoming his birth. For Robin
Oig's father, Lachlan M'Combich, or "son of my
friend" (his actual clan-surname being M'Gregor), had
been so called by the celebrated Rob Roy, because of
the particular friendship which had subsisted between
the grandsire of Robin and that renowned cateran.
Some people even say that Robin Oig derived his
Christian name from one as renowned in the wilds of
Loch Lomond as ever was his namesake, Robin Hood,
in the precincts of merry Sherwood. "Of such ances-
try," as James Boswell says, "who would not be
proud?" Robin Oig was proud accordingly; but his
frequent visits to England and to the Lowlands had
given him tact enough to know that pretensions which
still gave him a little right to distinction in his own
lonely glen might be both obnoxious and ridiculous
if preferred elsewhere. The pride of birth, therefore,
was like the miser's treasure, the secret subject of his
contemplation, but never exhibited to strangers as a
subject of boasting.

Many were the words of gratulation and good luck
which were bestowed on Robin Oig. The judges com-
mended his drove, especially Robin's own property,
which were the best of them. Some thrust out their
snuff-mulls for the parting pinch; others tendered the
doch-an-darroch, or parting-cup. All cried: "Good
luck travel out with you and come home with you.
Give you luck on the Saxon market—brave notes in
the leabhar-dhu (black pocket-book) and plenty of
English gold in the sporran" (pouch of goat-skin).

The bonny lasses made their adieus more modestly, and more than one, it was said, would have given her best brooch to be certain that it was upon her that his eye last rested as he turned towards the road.

Robin Oig had just given the preliminary "Hoo—hoo!" to urge forward the loiterers of the drove, when there was a cry behind him.

"Stay, Robin—bide a blink. Here is Janet of Toma-hourich—auld Janet, your father's sister."

"Plague on her, for an auld Highland witch and spaewife," said a farmer from the Carse of Stirling; "she'll cast some of her cantrips on the cattle."

"She canna do that," said another sapient of the same profession: "Robin Oig is no the lad to leave any of them without tying St. Mungo's knot on their tails, and that will put to her speed the best witch that ever flew over Dimayet upon a broomstick."

It may not be indifferent to the reader to know that the Highland cattle are peculiarly liable to be "taken," or infected, by spells and witchcraft, which judicious people guard against by knitting knots of peculiar complexity on the tuft of hair which terminates the animal's tail.

But the old woman who was the object of the farmer's suspicion seemed only busied about the drover, without paying any attention to the drove. Robin, on the contrary, appeared rather impatient of her presence.

"What auld-world fancy," he said, "has brought you so early from the ingle-side this morning, muhme? I am sure I bid you good-even, and had your God-speed, last night."

"And left me more siller than the useless old woman will use till you come back again, bird of my bosom," said the sibyl. "But it is little I would care for the food that nourishes me, or the fire that warms me, or for God's blessed sun itself, if aught but weal should happen to the grandson of my father. So let me walk the deasil round you, that you may go safe out into the far foreign land, and come safe home."

Robin Oig stopped, half embarrassed, half laughing, and signing to those around that he only complied with the old woman to soothe her humor. In the mean time, she traced around him, with wavering steps, the propitiation, which some have thought has been derived from the Druidical mythology. It consists, as is well known, in the person who makes the deasil walking three times round the person who is the object of the ceremony, taking care to move according to the course of the sun. At once, however, she stopped short, and exclaimed, in a voice of alarm and horror: "Grandson of my father, there is blood on your hand."

"Hush, for God's sake, aunt," said Robin Oig; "you will bring more trouble on yourself with this taishataragh (second sight) than you will be able to get out of for many a day."

The old woman only repeated with a ghastly look: "There is blood on your hand, and it is English blood. The blood of the Gael is richer and redder. Let us see—let us—"

Ere Robin Oig could prevent her, which, indeed, could only have been by positive violence, so hasty and peremptory were her proceedings, she had drawn from his side the dirk which lodged in the folds of his plaid, and held it up, exclaiming, altho the weapon gleamed clear and bright in the sun: "Blood, blood—Saxon blood again. Robin Oig M'Combich, go not this day to England!"

"Prutt, trutt," answered Robin Oig, "that will never

do neither; it would be next thing to running the
country. For shame, muhme, give me the dirk. You
cannot tell by the color the difference betwixt the blood
of a black bullock and a white one, and you speak
of knowing Saxon from Gaelic blood. All men have
their blood from Adam, muhme. Give me my skene-
dhu, and let me go on my road. I should have been
half-way to Stirling brig by this time. Give me my
dirk, and let me go."

"Never will I give it to you," said the old woman—
"never will I quit my hold on your plaid, unless you
promise me not to wear that unhappy weapon."

The women around him urged him also, saying few
of his aunt's words fell to the ground; and as the Lowland farmers continued to look moodily on the scene,
Robin Oig determined to close it at any sacrifice.

"Well, then," said the young drover, giving the scab-
bard of the weapon to Hugh Morrison, "you Low-
landers care nothing for these freats. Keep my dirk for
me. I cannot give it to you, because it was my
father's; but your drove follows ours, and I am content
it should be in your keeping, not in mine. Will this
do, muhme?"

"It must," said the old woman—"that is, if the Lowlander is mad enough to carry the knife."

The strong Westlandman laughed aloud.

"Goodwife," said he, "I am Hugh Morrison from
Glenae, come of the Manly Morrisons of auld lang-
syne, that never took short weapon against a man
in their lives. And neither needed they; they had their
broadswords, and I have this bit supple," showing a
formidable cudgel; "for dirking ower the board, I leave
that to John Highlandman. Ye needna snort, none of
you Highlanders, and you in especial, Robin. I'll keep

the bit knife, if you are feared for the auld spaewife's tale, and give it back to you whenever you want it."

Robin was not particularly pleased with some part of Hugh Morrison's speech; but he had learned in his travels more patience than belonged to his Highland constitution originally, and he accepted the service of the descendant of the Manly Morrisons, without finding fault with the rather depreciating manner in which it was offered.

"If he had not had his morning in his head, and been but a Dumfriesshire hog into the boot, he would have spoken more like a gentleman. But you cannot have more of a sow than a grumph. It's shame my father's knife should ever slash a haggis for the like of him."

Thus saying, but saying it in Gaelic, Robin drove on his cattle, and waved farewell to all behind him. He was in the greater haste, because he expected to join at Falkirk a comrade and brother in profession, with whom he proposed to travel in company.

Robin Oig's chosen friend was a young Englishman, Harry Wakefield by name, well known at every northern market, and in his way as much famed and honored as our Highland driver of bullocks. He was nearly six feet high, gallantly formed to keep the rounds at Smithfield, or maintain the ring at a wrestling match; and altho he might have been over-matched, perhaps, among the regular professors of the fancy, yet, as a yokel or rustic, or a chance customer, he was able to give a bellyful to any amateur of the pugilistic art. Doncaster races saw him in his glory, betting his guinea, and generally successfully; nor was there a main fought in Yorkshire, the feeders being persons of celebrity, at which he was not to be seen, if business permitted. But tho a "sprack" lad, and fond of pleasure and its haunts, Harry Wakefield was steady, and not the cautious Robin Oig M'Combich himself was more attentive to the main chance. His holidays were holidays indeed; but his days of work were dedicated to steady and persevering labor. In countenance and temper, Wakefield was the model of Old England's merry yeomen, whose cloth-yard shafts, in so many hundred battles, asserted her superiority over the nations, and whose good sabers, in our own time, are her cheapest and most assured defense. His mirth was readily excited; for, strong in limb and constitution, and fortunate in circumstances, he was disposed to be pleased with everything about him; and such difficulties as he might occasionally encounter were, to a man of his energy, rather matter of amusement than serious annoyance. With all the merits of a sanguine temper, our young English drover was not without his defects. He was irascible, sometimes to the verge of being quarrelsome; and perhaps not the less inclined to bring his disputes to a pugilistic decision, because he found few antagonists able to stand up to him in the boxing ring.

It is difficult to say how Harry Wakefield and Robin Oig first became intimates; but it is certain a close acquaintance had taken place betwixt them, altho they had apparently few common subjects of conversation or of interest, so soon as their talk ceased to be of bullocks. Robin Oig, indeed, spoke the English language rather imperfectly upon any other topics but stots and kyloes, and Harry Wakefield could never bring his broad Yorkshire tongue to utter a single word of Gaelic. It was in vain Robin spent a whole morning, during a walk over Minch Moor, in attempting to teach his companion to utter, with true precision, the shibboleth llhu, which is the Gaelic for a calf. From Traquair to Murder cairn, the hill rung with the discordant attempts of the Saxon upon the unmanageable monosyllable, and the heartfelt laugh which followed every failure. They had, however, better modes of awakening the echoes; for Wakefield could sing many a ditty to the praise of Moll, Susan, and Cicely, and Robin Oig had a particular gift at whistling interminable pibrochs through all their involutions, and, what was more agreeable to his companion's southern ear, knew many of the northern airs, both lively and pathetic, to which Wakefield learned to pipe a bass. Thus, tho Robin could hardly have comprehended his companion's stories about horse-racing, and cock-fighting, or fox-hunting, and altho his own legends of clan-fights, and creaghs, varied with talk of Highland goblins and fairy folk, would have been caviare to his companion, they contrived nevertheless to find a degree of pleasure in each other's company, which had for three years back induced them to join company and travel together, when the direction of their journey permitted. Each, indeed, found his advantage in this companionship; for where could the Englishman have found a guide through the Western Highlands like Robin Oig M'Combich? and when they were on what Harry called the *right* side of the Border, his patronage, which was extensive, and his purse, which was heavy, were at all times at the service of his Highland friend, and on many occasions his liberality did him genuine yeoman's service.

Chapter II

Were ever two such loving friends!—
  How could they disagree?
Oh, thus it was, he loved him dear,
  And thought how to requite him,
And having no friend left but he,
  He did resolve to fight him.
                    —*Duke upon Duke.*

The pair of friends had traversed with their usual
cordiality the grassy wilds of Liddesdale, and crossed
the opposite part of Cumberland, emphatically called
The Waste. In these solitary regions the cattle under
the charge of our drovers derived their subsistence
chiefly by picking their food as they went along the
drove-road, or sometimes by the tempting opportunity
of a "start and owerloup," or invasion of the neighboring pasture, where an occasion presented itself. But
now the scene changed before them; they were descending towards a fertile and inclosed country, where
no such liberties could be taken with impunity, or
without a previous arrangement and bargain with the
possessors of the ground. This was more especially the
case, as a great northern fair was upon the eve of taking
place, where both the Scotch and English drover expected to dispose of a part of their cattle, which it
was desirable to produce in the market rested and in
good order. Fields were therefore difficult to be
obtained, and only upon high terms. This necessity
occasioned a temporary separation betwixt the two
friends who went to bargain, each as he could, for the
separate accommodation of his herd. Unhappily it
chanced that both of them, unknown to each other,
thought of bargaining for the ground they wanted on
the property of a country gentleman of some fortune,
whose estate lay in the neighborhood. The English

drover applied to the bailiff on the property, who was known to him. It chanced that the Cumbrian squire, who had entertained some suspicions of his manager's honesty, was taking occasional measures to ascertain how far they were well founded, and had desired that any inquiries about his inclosures, with a view to occupy them for a temporary purpose, should be referred to himself. As, however, Mr. Ireby had gone the day before upon a journey of some miles' distance to the northward, the bailiff chose to consider the check upon his full powers as for the time removed, and concluded that he should best consult his master's interest, and perhaps his own, in making an agreement with Harry Wakefield.

Meanwhile, ignorant of what his comrade was doing, Robin Oig, on his side, chanced to be overtaken by a goodlooking, smart little man upon a pony, most knowingly hogged and cropped, as was then fashion, the rider wearing tight leather breeches and long-necked bright spurs. This cavalier asked one or two pertinent questions about markets and the price of stock. So Robin, seeing him a well-judging, civil gentleman, took the freedom to ask him whether he could let him know if there was any grass-land to be let in that neighborhood, for the temporary accommodation of his drove. He could not have put the question to more willing ears. The gentleman of the buckskins was the proprietor with whose bailiff Harry Wakefield had dealt, or was in the act of dealing.

"Thou art in good luck, my canny Scot," said Mr. Ireby, "to have spoken to me, for I see thy cattle have done their day's work, and I have at my disposal the only field within three miles that is to be let in these parts."

"The drove can pe gang two, three, four miles very pratty weel indeed," said the cautious Highlander; "put what would his honor pe axing for the peasts pe the head, if she was to tak the park for twa or three days?"

"We won't differ, Sawney, if you let me have six stots for winterers, in the way of reason."

"And which peasts wad your honor pe for having?"

"Why, let me see—the two black—the dun one—yon doddy—him with the twisted horn—the brockit. How much by the head?"

"Ah," said Robin, "your honor is a shudge—a real shudge: I couldna have set off the pest six peasts petter myself, me that ken them as if they were my pairns, puir things."

"Well, how much per head, Sawney?" continued Mr. Ireby.

"It was the high markets at Doune and Falkirk," answered Robin.

And thus the conversation proceeded, until they had agreed on the prix juste for the bullocks, the squire throwing in the temporary accommodation of the inclosure for the cattle into the boot, and Robin making, as he thought, a very good bargain, provided the grass was but tolerable. The squire walked his pony alongside of the drove, partly to show him the way, and see him put into possession of the field, and partly to learn the latest news of the northern markets.

They arrived at the field, and the pasture seemed excellent. But what was their surprize when they saw the bailiff quietly inducting the cattle of Harry Wakefield into the grassy goshen which had just been assigned to those of Robin Oig M'Combich by the proprietor himself! Squire Ireby set spurs to his horse, dashed up to his servant, and learning what had passed between the parties, briefly informed the English drover that his bailiff had let the ground without his authority, and that he might seek grass for his cattle wherever he would, since he was to get none there. At the same time he rebuked his servant severely for having transgressed his commands, and ordered him instantly to assist in ejecting the hungry and weary cattle of Harry Wakefield, which were just beginning to enjoy a meal of unusual plenty, and to introduce those of his comrade, whom the English drover now began to consider as a rival.

The feelings which arose in Wakefield's mind would have induced him to resist Mr. Ireby's decision; but every Englishman has a tolerably accurate sense of law and justice, and John Fleecebumpkin, the bailiff, having acknowledged that he had exceeded his commission, Wakefield saw nothing else for it than to collect his hungry and disappointed charge, and drive them on to seek quarters elsewhere. Robin Oig saw what had happened with regret, and hastened to offer to his English friend to share with him the disputed possession. But Wakefield's pride was severely hurt, and he answered disdainfully. "Take it all, man—take it all; never make two bites of a cherry. Thou canst talk over the gentry, and bear a plain man's eye. Out upon you, man; I would not kiss any man's dirty latchets for leave to bake in his oven."

Robin Oig, sorry but not surprised at his comrade's displeasure, hastened to entreat his friend to wait but an hour till he had gone to the squire's house to receive payment for the cattle he had sold, and he would come back and help him to drive the cattle into some con-

venient place of rest, and explain to him the whole
mistake they had both of them fallen into.

But the Englishman continued indignant. "Thou hast
been selling, hast thou? Ay—ay, thou is a cunning lad
for kenning the hours of bargaining. Go to the devil
with thyself, for I will ne'er see thy fause loon's
visage again; thou should be ashamed to look me in
the face."

"I am ashamed to look no man in the face," said
Robin Oig, something moved; "and, moreover, I will
look you in the face this blessed day, if you will bide
at the clachan down yonder."

"Mayhap you had as well keep away," said his comrade; and turning his back on his former friend, he
collected his unwilling associates, assisted by the bailiff,
who took some real and some affected interest in seeing
Wakefield accommodated.

After spending some time in negotiating with more
than one of the neighboring farmers, who could not,
or would not, afford the accommodation desired, Henry
Wakefield at last, and in his necessity, accomplished
his point by means of the landlord of the alehouse at
which Robin Oig and he had agreed to pass the night,
when they first separated from each other. Mine host
was content to let him turn his cattle on a piece of barren
moor, at a price little less than the bailiff had asked
for the disputed inclosure, and the wretchedness of the
pasture, as well as the price paid for it, were set down
as exaggerations of the breach of faith and friendship
of his Scottish crony. This turn of Wakefield's passions
was encouraged by the bailiff, who had his own reasons
for being offended against poor Robin, as having been
the unwitting cause of his falling into disgrace with his
master, as well as by the inkeeper, and two or three

chance guests, who stimulated the drover in his resentment against his quondam associate—some from the ancient grudge against the Scots, which, when it exists anywhere, is to be found lurking in the Border counties, and some from the general love of mischief, which characterizes mankind in all ranks of life, to the honor of Adam's children be it spoken. Good John Barleycorn also, who always heightens and exaggerates the prevailing passions, be they angry or kindly, was not wanting in his offices on this occasion; and confusion to false friends and hard masters was pledged in more than one tankard.

In the mean while, Mr. Ireby found some amusement in detaining the northern drover at his ancient hall. He caused a cold round of beef to be placed before the Scot in the butler's pantry, together with a foaming tankard of home-brewed, and took pleasure in seeing the hearty appetite with which these unwonted edibles were discussed by Robin Oig M'Combich. The squire himself, lighting his pipe, compounded between his patrician dignity and his love of agricultural gossip, by walking up and down while he conversed with his guest.

"I passed another drove," said the squire, "with one of your countrymen behind them; they were something less beast than your drove, doddies most of them; a big man was with them—none of your kilts tho, but a decent pair of breeches. D'ye know who he may be?"

"Hout aye, that might, could, and would be Hughie Morrison; I didna think he could hae peen sae weel up. He has made a day on us; but his Argyleshires will have wearied shanks. How far was he pehind?"

"I think about six or seven miles," answered the

squire, "for I passed them at the Christenbury Crag, and I overtook you at the Hollan Bush. If his beasts be leg-weary, he will be maybe selling bargains."

"Na—na, Hughie Morrison is no the man for pargains; ye maun come to some Highland body like Robin Oig hersell for the like of these. Put I maun pe wishing you goot night, and twenty of them let alane ane, and I maun down to the clachan to see if the lad Harry Waakfelt is out of his humdudgeons yet."

The party at the alehouse were still in full talk, and the treachery of Robin Oig still the theme of conversation, when the supposed culprit entered the apartment. His arrival, as usually happens in such a case, put an instant stop to the discussion of which he had furnished the subject, and he was received by the company assembled with that chilling silence which, more than a thousand exclamations, tells an intruder that he is unwelcome. Surprized and offended, but not appalled, by the reception which he experienced, Robin entered with an undaunted and even a haughty air, attempted no greeting, as he saw he was received with none, and placed himself by the side of the fire, a little apart from a table at which Harry Wakefield, the bailiff, and two or three other persons were seated. The ample Cumbrian kitchen would have afforded plenty of room, even for a larger separation.

Robin, thus seated, proceeded to light his pipe and call for a pint of twopenny.

"We have no twopence ale," answered Ralph Heskett, the landlord; "but, as thou find'st thy own tobacco, it's like thou mayst find thy own liquor too; it's the wont of thy country, I wot."

"Shame, goodman," said the landlady, a blythe, bustling housewife, hastening herself to supply the guest with liquor. "Thou knowest well enow what the strange man wants, and it's thy trade to be civil, man. Thou shouldst know, that if the Scot likes a small pot, he pays a sure penny."

Without taking any notice of this nuptial dialog, the Highlander took the flagon in his hand, and addressing the company generally, drank the interesting toast of "Good markets," to the party assembled.

"The better that the wind blew fewer dealers from the north," said one of the farmers, "and fewer Highland runts to eat up the English meadows."

"Saul of my pody, put you are wrang there, my friend," answered Robin, with composure; "it is your fat Englishmen that eat up our Scots cattle, puir things.'

"I wish there was a summat to eat up their drovers," said another; "a plain Englishman canna make bread with a kenning of them."

"Or an honest servant keep his master's favor, but they will come sliding in between him and the sunshine," said the bailiff.

"If these pe jokes," said Robin Oig, with the same composure, "there is ower mony jokes upon one man."

"It is no joke, but downright earnest," said the bailiff. "Harkye, Mr. Robin Ogg, or whatever is your name, it's right we should tell you that we are all of one opinion, and that is, that you, Mr. Robin Ogg, have behaved to our friend, Mr. Harry Wakefield here. like a raff and a blackguard."

"Nae doubt—nae doubt," answered Robin, with great composure; "and you are a set of very pretty judges, for whose prains or pehavior I wad not gie a pinch of sneeshing. If Mr. Harry Waakfelt kens where he is wranged, he kens where he may be righted."

"He speaks truth," said Wakefield, who had listened to what passed, divided between the offense which he had taken at Robin's late behavior and the revival of his habitual feelings of regard.

He now rose and went towards Robin, who got up from his seat as he approached and held out his hand.

"That's right, Harry—go it—serve him out," responded on all sides—"tip him the nailer—show him the mill."

"Hold your peace all of you, and be—," said Wakefield; and then addressing his comrade, he took him by the extended hand, with something alike of respect and defiance. "Robin," he said, "thou hast used me ill enough this day; but if you mean, like a frank fellow, to shake hands, and take a tussle for love on the sod, why, I'll forgive thee, man, and we shall be better friends than ever."

"And would it no pe petter to pe cood friends without more of the matter?" said Robin; "we will be much petter friendships with our panes hale than broken."

Harry Wakefield dropped the hand of his friend, or rather threw it from him.

"I did not think I had been keeping company for three years with a coward."

"Coward pelongs to none of my name," said Robin, whose eyes began to kindle, but keeping the command of his temper. "It was no coward's legs or hands, Harry Waakfelt, that drew you out of the fords of Frew, when you was drifting ower the plack rock, and every eel in the river expected his share of you."

"And that is true enough, too," said the Englishman, struck by the appeal.

"Adzooks!" exclaimed the bailiff; "sure Harry Wakefield, the nattiest lad at Whitson Tryste, Wooler Fair,

Carlisle Sands, or Stagshaw Bank, is not going to show white feather? Ah, this comes of living so long with kilts and bonnets; men forget the use of their daddles."

"I may teach you, Master Fleecebumpkin, that I have not lost the use of mine," said Wakefield, and then went on: "This will never do, Robin. We must have a turn-up, or we shall be the talk of the countryside. I'll be d—d if I hurt thee. I'll put on the gloves gin thou like. Come, stand forward like a man."

"To be peaten like a dog," said Robin; "is there any reason in that? If you think I have done you wrong, I'll go before your shudge, tho I neither know his law nor his language."

A general cry of "No, no—no law, no lawyer! A bellyful and be friends!" was echoed by the bystanders.

"But," continued Robin, "if I am to fight, I have no skill to fight like a jackanapes, with hands and nails."

"How would you fight then?" said his antagonist; "tho I am thinking it would be hard to bring you to the scratch anyhow."

"I would fight with proadswords, and sink point on the first plood drawn, like a gentlemans."

A loud shout of laughter followed the proposal, which indeed had rather escaped from poor Robin's swelling heart than been the dictate of his sober judgment.

"Gentleman, quotha!" was echoed on all sides, with a shout of unextinguishable laughter; "a very pretty gentleman, God wot. Canst get two swords for the gentleman to fight with, Ralph Heskett?"

"No, but I can send to the armory at Carlisle, and lend them two forks, to be making shift with in the mean time."

"Tush, man," said another, "the bonny Scots come

into the world with the blue bonnet on their heads,
and dirk and pistol at their belt."

"Best send post," said Mr. Fleecebumpkin, "to the
squire of Corby Castle, to come and stand second to
the *gentleman*."

In the midst of this torrent of general ridicule, the
Highlander instinctively griped beneath the folds of
his plaid.

"But it's better not," he said in his own language.
"A hundred curses on the swine-eaters, who know
neither decency nor civility!"

"Make room, the pack of you," he said, advancing
to the door.

But his former friend interposed his sturdy bulk, and
opposed his leaving the house; and when Robin Oig
attempted to make his way by force, he hit him down
on the floor, with as much ease as a boy bowls down
a ninepin.

"A ring—a ring!" was now shouted, until the dark
rafters, and the hams that hung on them, trembled
again, and the very platters on the "bink" clattered
against each other. "Well done, Harry"—"Give it him
home, Harry"—"Take care of him now, he sees his
own blood!"

Such were the exclamations, while the Highlander,
starting from the ground, all his coldness and caution
lost in frantic rage, sprung at his antagonist with the
fury, the activity, and the vindicative purpose of an
incensed tiger-cat. But when could rage encounter
science and temper? Robin Oig again went down in the
unequal contest; and as the blow was necessarily a
severe one, he lay motionless on the floor of the
kitchen.

The landlady ran to offer some aid; but Mr. Fleecebumpkin would not permit her to approach. "Let him alone," he said, "he will come to within time, and come up to the scratch again. He has not got half his broth yet."

"He has got all I mean to give him, tho," said his antagonist, whose heart began to relent towards his old associate; "and I would rather by half give the rest to yourself, Mr. Fleecebumpkin, for you pretend to know a thing or two, and Robin had not art enough even to peel before setting to, but fought with his plaid dangling about him. Stand up, Robin, my man, all friends now, and let me hear the man that will speak a word against you, or your country, for your sake."

Robin Oig was still under the dominion of his passion, and eager to renew the onset; but being withheld on the one side by the peacemaking Dame Heskett, and on the other aware that Wakefield no longer meant to renew the combat, his fury sunk into gloomy sullenness.

"Come—come, never grudge so much at it, man," said the brave-spirited Englishman, with the placability of his country; "shake hands, and we will be better friends than ever."

"Friends!" exclaimed Robin Oig with strong emphasis—"friends! Never. Look to yourself, Harry Waakfelt."

"Then the curse of Cromwell on your proud Scots stomach, as the man says in the play, and you may do your worst, and be d—d; for one man can say nothing more to another after a tussle, than that he is sorry for it."

On these terms the friends parted. Robin Oig drew out in silence a piece of money, threw it on the table, and then left the alehouse. But, turning at the door,

he shook his hand at Wakefield, pointing with his fore-
finger upwards, in a manner which might imply either
a threat or a caution. He then disappeared in the
moonlight.

Some words passed after his departure between the
bailiff, who piqued himself on being a little of a bully,
and Harry Wakefield, who, with generous inconsistency,
was now not indisposed to begin a new combat in defense of Robin Oig's reputation, "altho he could not
use his daddles like an Englishman, as it did not come
natural to him."

But Dame Heskett prevented this second quarrel
from coming to a head by her peremptory interference.
"There should be no more fighting in her house," she
said; "there had been too much already. And you,
Mr. Wakefield, may live to learn," she added, "what it
is to make a deadly enemy out of a good friend."

"Pshaw, dame! Robin Oig is an honest fellow, and
will never keep malice."

"Do not trust to that: you do not know the dour
temper of the Scots, tho you have dealt with them so
often. I have a right to know them, my mother being
a Scot."

"And so is well seen on her daughter," said Ralph
Heskett.

This nuptial sarcasm gave the discourse another turn;
fresh customers entered the taproom or kitchen, and
others left it. The conversation turned on the expected markets, and the reports of prices from different parts both of Scotland and England; treaties were
commenced, and Harry Wakefield was lucky enough to
find a chap for a part of his drove, and at a very
considerable profit—an event of consequence more than

sufficient to blot out all remembrances of the unpleasant scuffle in the earlier part of the day.

But there remained one party from whose mind that recollection could not have been wiped away by the possession of every head of cattle betwixt Esk and Eden. This was Robin Oig M'Combich. "That I should have had no weapon," he said, "and for the first time in my life! Blighted be the tongue that bids the Highlander part with the dirk. The dirk hae! the English blood! My muhme's word—when did her word fall to the ground?"

The recollection of the fatal prophecy confirmed the deadly intention which instantly sprang up in his mind.

"Ha! Morrison cannot be many miles behind; and if it were an hundred, what then?"

His impetuous spirit had now a fixed purpose and motive of action, and he turned the light foot of his country towards the wilds, through which he knew, by Mr. Ireby's report, that Morrison was advancing. His mind was wholly engrossed by the sense of injury— injury sustained from a friend, and by the desire of vengeance on one whom he now accounted his most bitter enemy. The treasured ideas of self-importance and self-opinion—of ideal birth and quality, had become more precious to him, like the hoard to the miser, because he could only enjoy them in secret. But that hoard was pillaged; the idols which he had secretly worshipped had been desecrated and profaned. Insulted, abused and beaten, he was no longer worthy, in his own opinion, of the name he bore, or the lineage which he belonged to; nothing was left to him—nothing but revenge; and, as the reflection added a galling spur to every step, he determined it should be as sudden and signal as the offense.

When Robin Oig left the door of the alehouse, seven
or eight English miles at least lay betwixt Morrison
and him. The advance of the former was slow, limited
by the sluggish pace of his cattle; the last left behind
him stubble-field and hedge-row, crag and dark heath,
all glittering with frost-rime in the broad November
moonlight, at the rate of six miles an hour. And now
the distant lowing of Morrison's cattle is heard; and
now they are seen creeping like moles in size and
slowness of motion on the broad face of the moor;
and now he meets them, passes them, and stops their
conductor.

"May good betide us," said the Southlander. "Is
this you, Robin M'Combich, or your wraith?"

"It is Robin Oig M'Combich," answered the Highlander, "and it is not. But never mind that, put pe
giving me the skene-dhu."

"What, you are for back to the Highlands! The
devil! Have you selt all off before the fair? This
beats all for quick markets."

"I have not sold—I am not going north. May pe I
will never go north again. Give me pack my dirk,
Hugh Morrison, or there will pe words between us."

"Indeed, Robin, I'll be better advised before I gie
it back to you; it is a wanchancy weapon in a Highlandman's hand, and I am thinking you will be about
some barns-breaking."

"Prutt, trutt! let me have my weapon," said Robin
Oig, impatiently.

"Hooly and fairly," said his well-meaning friend.
"I'll tell you what will do better than these dirking
doings. Ye ken Highlander, and Lowlander, and Bor-
dermen are a' ae man's bairns when you are over the
Scots dyke. See, the Eskdale callants, and fighting

Charlie of Liddesdale, and the Lockerby lads, and the
four Dandies of Lustruther, and a ween mair gray
plaids are coming up behind; and if you are wranged,
there is the hand of a Manly Morrison, we'll see you
righted, if Carlisle and Stanwix baith took up the
feud."

"To tell you the truth," said Robin Oig, desirous
of eluding the suspicions of his friend, "I have enlisted
with a party of the Black Watch, and must march off
tomorrow morning."

"Enlisted! Were you mad or drunk? You must
buy yourself off. I can lend you twenty notes, and
twenty to that, if the drove sell."

"I thank you—thank ye, Hughie; but I go with good-
will the gate that I am going; so the dirk—the dirk!"

"There it is for you then, since less wunna serve.
But think on what I was saying. Waes me, it will be
sair news in the braes of Balquidder, that Robin Oig
M'Combich should have run an ill gate, and ta'en on."

"Ill news in Balquidder, indeed!" echoed poor Robin;
"but Cot speed you, Hughie, and send you good mar-
cats. Ye winna meet with Robin Oig again, either at
tryste or fair."

So saying he shook hastily the hand of his acquaintance, and set out in the direction from which he had
advanced, with the spirit of his former pace.

"There is something wrang with the lad," muttered
the Morrison to himself; "but we will maybe see better into it the morn's morning."

But long ere the morning dawned, the catastrophe
of our tale had taken place. It was two hours after
the affray had happened, and it was totally forgotten
by almost every one, when Robin Oig returned to
Heskett's inn. The place was filled at once by various

sorts of men and with noises corresponding to their character. There were the grave low sounds of men engaged in busy traffic, with the laugh, the song, and the riotous jest of those who had nothing to do but to enjoy themselves. Among the last was Harry Wakefield, who, amidst a grinning group of smock-frocks, hobnailed shoes, and jolly English physiognomies, was trolling forth the old ditty:

> "What tho my name be Roger,
> Who drives the plow and cart—"

when he was interrupted by a well-known voice saying in a high and stern voice, marked by the sharp Highland accent, "Harry Waakfelt, if you be a man, stand up!"

"What is the matter?—what is it?" the guests demanded of each other.

"It is only a d—d Scotsman," said Fleecebumpkin, who was by this time very drunk, "whom Harry Wakefield helped to his broth today, who is now come to have his cauld kail het again."

"Harry Waakfelt," repeated the same ominous summons, "stand up, if you be a man!"

There is something in the tone of deep and concentrated passion which attracts attention and imposes awe, even by the very sound. The guests shrunk back on every side, and gazed at the Highlander as he stood in the middle of them, his brows bent, and his features rigid with resolution.

"I will stand up with all my heart, Robin, my boy, but it shall be to shake hands with you, and drink down all unkindness. It is not the fault of your heart, man, that you don't know how to clench your hands."

By this time he stood opposite to his antagonist; his open and unsuspecting look strangely contrasted with the stern purpose which gleamed wild, dark, and vindicative in the eyes of the Highlander.

" 'Tis not thy fault, man, that, not having the luck to be an Englishman, thou canst not fight more than a school-girl."

"I *can* fight," answered Robin Oig, sternly but calmly, "and you shall know it. You, Harry Waakfelt, showed me today how the Saxon churls fight; I show you now how the Highland duiniè-wassel fights."

He seconded the word with the action, and plunged the dagger, which he suddenly displayed, into the broad breast of the English yeoman, with such fatal certainty and force that the hilt made a hollow sound against the breast-bone, and the double-edged point split the very heart of his victim. Harry Wakefield fell and expired with a single groan. His assassin next seized the bailiff by the collar, and offered the bloody poniard to his throat, whilst dread and surprize rendered the man incapable of defense.

"It was very just to lay you beside him," he said, "but the blood of a base pickthank shall never mix on my father's dirk with that of a brave man."

As he spoke, he cast the man from him with so much force that he fell on the floor, while Robin, with his other hand, threw the fatal weapon into the blazing turf-fire.

"There," he said, "take me who likes, and let fire cleanse blood if it can."

The cause of astonishment still continuing, Robin Oig asked for a peace-officer, and a constable having stepped out, he surrendered himself to his custody.

"A bloody night's work you have made of it," said the constable.

"Your own fault," said the Highlander. "Had you

kept his hands off of me twa hours since, he would
have been now as well and merry as he was two minutes since."

"It must be sorely answered," said the peace-officer.

"Never you mind that. Death pays all debts; it will
pay that too."

The horror of the bystanders began now to give
way to indignation; and the sight of a favorite companion murdered in the midst of them, the provocation
being, in their opinion, so utterly inadequate to the
excess of vengeance, might have induced them to kill
the perpetrator of the deed even upon the very spot.
The constable, however, did his duty on this occasion,
and, with the assistance of some of the more reasonable
persons present, procured horses to guard the prisoner
to Carlisle, to abide his doom at the next assizes.
While the escort was preparing, the prisoner neither
expressed the least interest nor attempted the slightest
reply. Only, before he was carried from the fatal
apartment, he desired to look at the dead body, which,
raised from the floor, had been deposited upon the
large table (at the head of which Harry Wakefield had
presided but a few minutes before, full of life, vigor,
and animation), until the surgeons should examine the
mortal wound. The face of the corpse was decently
covered with a napkin. To the surprize and horror
of the bystanders, which displayed itself in a general
"Ah!" drawn through clenched teeth and half-shut lips,
Robin Oig removed the cloth, and gazed with a mourn-
ful but steady eye on the lifeless visage, which had
been so lately animated, that the smile of good-humored
confidence in his own strength, of conciliation at once
and contempt towards his enemy, still curled his lip.
While those present expected that the wound, which

had so lately flooded the apartment with gore, would send forth fresh streams at the touch of the homicide, Robin Oig replaced the covering with the brief exclamation, "He was a pretty man!"

My story is nearly ended. The unfortunate Highlander stood his trial at Carlisle. I was myself present, and as a young Scottish lawyer, or barrister at least, and reputed a man of some quality, the politeness of the sheriff of Cumberland offered me a place on the bench. The facts of the case were proved in the manner I have related them; and whatever might be at first the prejudice of the audience against a crime so un-English as that of assassination from revenge, yet when the rooted national prejudices of the prisoner had been explained, which made him consider himself as stained with indelible dishonor when subjected to personal violence, when his previous patience, moderation, and endurance were considered, the generosity of the English audience was inclined to regard his crime as the wayward aberration of a false idea of honor rather than as flowing from a heart naturally savage, or perverted by habitual vice. I shall never forget the charge of the venerable judge to the jury, altho not at that time liable to be much affected either by that which was eloquent or pathetic.

"We have had," he said, "in the previous part of our duty (alluding to some former trials), to discuss crimes which infer disgust and abhorrence, while they call down the well-merited vengeance of the law. It is now our still more melancholy task to apply its salutary tho severe enactments to a case of a very singular character, in which the crime, for a crime it is, and a deep one, arose less out of the malevolence of the heart than the error of the understanding—less from any idea of committing wrong than from an unhappily perverted notion of that which is right. Here we have two men, highly esteemed, it has been stated, in the rank of life, and attached, it seems, to each other as friends, one of whose lives has been already sacrificed to a punctillio, and the other is about to prove the vengeance of the offended law; and yet both may claim our commiseration at least, as men acting in ignorance of each other's national prejudices, and unhappily misguided rather than voluntarily erring from the path of right conduct.

"In the original cause of the misunderstanding, we must in justice give the right to the prisoner at the bar. He had acquired possession of the inclosure, which was the object of competition, by a legal contract with the proprietor, Mr. Ireby; and yet, when accosted with reproaches undeserved in themselves, and galling doubtless to a temper at least sufficiently susceptible of passion, he offered notwithstanding to yield up half his acquisition, for the sake of peace and good neighborhood, and his amicable proposal was rejected with scorn. Then follows the scene at Mr. Heskett the publican's, and you will observe how the stranger was treated by the deceased, and, I am sorry to observe, by those around, who seem to have urged him in a manner which was aggravating in the highest degree. While he asked for peace and for composition, and offered submission to a magistrate, or to a mutual arbiter, the prisoner was insulted by a whole company, who seem on this occasion to have forgotten the national maxim of 'fair play'; and while attempting to escape from the place in peace, he was intercepted, struck down, and beaten to the effusion of his blood.

"Gentlemen of the jury, it was with some impatience that I heard my learned brother, who opened the case for the crown, give an unfavorable turn to the prisoner's conduct on this occasion. He said the prisoner was afraid to encounter his antagonist in fair fight, or to submit to the laws of the ring; and that, therefore, like a cowardly Italian, he had recourse to his fatal stiletto, to murder the man whom he dared not meet in manly encounter. I observed the prisoner shrink from this part of the accusation with the abhorrence natural to a brave man; and as I would wish to make my words impressive when I point his real crime, I must secure his opinion of my impartiality by rebutting everything that seems to me a false accusation. There can be no doubt that the prisoner is a man of resolution—too much resolution. I wish to Heaven that he had less, or rather that he had had a better education to regulate it.

"Gentlemen, as to the laws my brother talks of, they may be known in the bull-ring, or the bear-garden, or the cock-pit, but they are not known here. Or, if they should be so far admitted as furnishing a species of proof that no malice was intended in this sort of combat, from which fatal accidents do sometimes arise, it can only be so admitted when both parties are in *pari casu,* equally acquainted with, and equally willing to refer themselves to, that species of arbitrament. But will it be contended that a man of superior rank and education is to be subjected, or is obliged to subject himself, to this coarse and brutal strife, perhaps in opposition to a younger, stronger, or more skilful opponent? Certainly even the pugilistic code, if founded upon the fair play of Merry Old England, as my brother alleges it to be, can contain nothing so preposterous. And, gentlemen of the jury, if the laws would support an English gentleman, wearing, we will suppose, his sword, in defending himself by force against a violent personal aggression of the nature offered to this prisoner, they will not less protect a foreigner and a stranger, involved in the same unpleasing circumstances. If, therefore, gentlemen of the jury, when thus pressed by a *vis major,* the object of obloquy to a whole company, and of direct violence from one at least, and, as he might reasonably apprehend, from more, the panel had produced the weapon which his countrymen, as we are informed, generally carry about their persons, and the same unhappy circumstance had ensued which you have heard detailed in evidence, I could not in my conscience have asked from you a verdict of murder. The prisoner's personal defense might indeed, even in that case, have gone more or less beyond the *moderamen inculpatæ tutelæ* spoken of by lawyers, but the punishment incurred would have been that of manslaughter, not of murder. I beg leave to add, that I should have thought this milder species of charge was demanded in the case supposed, notwithstanding the statute of James I. cap. 8, which takes the case of slaughter by stabbing with a short weapon, even without malice prepense, out of the benefit of clergy. For this statute of stabbing, as it is termed, arose out of a temporary cause; and as the real guilt is the same, whether the slaughter be committed by the dagger or by sword or pistol, the benignity of the modern law places them all on the same, or nearly the same, footing.

"But, gentlemen of the jury, the pinch of the case lies in the interval of two hours interposed betwixt the reception of the injury and the fatal retaliation. In

the heat of affray and *chaude mêlée*, law, compassion-
ating the infirmities of humanity, makes allowance for
the passions which rule such a stormy moment—for
the sense of present pain, for the apprehension of
further injury, for the difficulty of ascertaining with
due accuracy the precise degree of violence which is
necessary to protect the person of the individual, without annoying or injuring the assailant more than is
absolutely necessary. But the time necessary to walk
twelve miles, however speedily performed, was an interval sufficient for the prisoner to have recollected himself; and the violence with which he carried his purpose
into effect, with so many circumstances of deliberate
determination, could neither be induced by the passion
of anger nor that of fear. It was the purpose and the
act of predetermined revenge, for which law neither
can, will, nor ought to have sympathy or allowance.

"It is true, we may repeat to ourselves, in alleviation
of this poor man's unhappy action, that his case is a
very peculiar one. The country which he inhabits was,
in the days of many now alive, inaccessible to the laws
not only of England, which have not even yet pene-
trated thither, but to those to which our neighbors of
Scotland are subjected, and which must be supposed
to be, and no doubt actually are, founded upon the
general principles of justice and equity which pervade
every civilized country. Amongst their mountains, as
among the North American Indians, the various tribes
were wont to make war upon each other, so that each
man was obliged to go armed for his own protection.
These men, from the ideas which they entertained of
their own descent and of their own consequence, regarded themselves as so many cavaliers or men-at-arms,
rather than as the peasantry of a peaceful country.

Those laws of the ring, as my brother terms them, were unknown to the race of warlike mountaineers; that decision of quarrels by no other weapons than those which nature has given every man must to them have seemed as vulgar and as preposterous as to the noblesse of France. Revenge, on the other hand, must have been as familiar to their habits of society as to those of the Cherokees or Mohawks. It is indeed, as described by Bacon, at bottom a kind of wild untutored justice; for the fear of retaliation must withhold the hands of the oppressor where there is no regular law to check daring violence. But tho all this may be granted and tho we may allow that, such having been the case of the Highlands in the days of the prisoner's fathers, many of the opinions and sentiments must still continue to influence the present generation, it cannot, and ought not, even in this most painful case, to alter the administration of the law, either in your hands, gentlemen of the jury, or in mine. The first object of civilization is to place the general protection of the law, equally administered, in the room of that wild justice which every man cut and carved for himself, according to the length of his sword and the strength of his arm. The law says to the subjects, with a voice only inferior to that of the Deity, 'vengeance is mine.' The instant that there is time for passion to cool and reason to interpose, an injured party must become aware that the law assumes the exclusive cognizance of the right and wrong betwixt the parties, and opposes her inviolable buckler to every attempt of the private party to right himself. I repeat, that this unhappy man ought personally to be the object rather of our pity than our abhorrence, for he failed in his ignorance and from mistaken notions of honor. But his crime is not the less that of murder, gentlemen, and, in your high and important office, it is your duty so to find. Englishmen have their angry passions as well as Scots; and should this man's action remain unpunished, you may unsheath, under various pretenses, a thousand daggers betwixt the Land's End and the Orkneys."

The venerable judge thus ended what, to judge by his apparent emotion, and by the tears which filled his eyes, was really a painful task. The jury, according to his instructions, brought in a verdict of Guilty; and Robin Oïg M'Combich, alias M'Gregor, was sentenced to death, and left for execution, which took place accordingly. He met his fate with great firmness, and acknowledged the justice of his sentence. But he repelled indignantly the observations of those who accused him of attacking an unarmed man. "I give a life for the life I took," he said, "and what can I do more?"

KARI AASEN IN HEAVEN

By Johan Bojer

Kari Aasen was married to Peter Aasen. They had together made the clearing for their little farm, and many an evening had lain down weary in their big, wide bed. Like two good plow-horses they had pulled hard and easily side by side, and they could not imagine the possibility of anything happening to the one of them that did not happen to the other too. It is true that when Peter had been to the town he came home drunk and beat his wife; but the next day he was so remorseful that he beat himself.

One day Kari took to her bed, and Peter sat on a stool beside her, and asked over and over again whether she did not feel better. She kept on answering, too, that now, thank God, she felt better; but at last Peter saw that his wife was so ill that it would be better to go for the priest.

That night Kari suddenly saw that it was not Peter who sat by her bedside, but a man clothed in white garments, who had come to fetch her; and she burst into tears and pleaded: "No, no! I would rather stay with Peter!"

"What do you say?" asked her husband, who was sitting watching beside her.

But at last Kari saw the white-clad figure spread his wings, and heard him say: "Now, Kari, you must

98

come with me." And Kari was obliged to go with him, for he took her up in his arms. They went out of the cottage and up into the air, and the Aasen buildings grew smaller and smaller; past both the sun and the stars, and much, much farther. Then Kari began once more to whimper and complain, but the stranger dried her tears and said, "Be glad of heart, for now all your troubles are at an end."

"Oh, I was so happy where I was," said Kari. "And Peter, will he be left there all alone, old and worn out as he is?"

"God will take care of him," said the stranger. "Rejoice that you will soon be in Paradise."

Kari tried to rejoice, for she had always intended to manage so that she would go to heaven when she died; but at the same time she could not help wondering whether Peter would remember to mend the sheep's tether.

At last they stopped at a great, golden gate, much larger than the gate of the magistrate's house, and passed through a garden where a number of children were playing. Among these Kari recognized a neighbor's child that had died of scarlet fever, and she said to herself: "If ever I go back to earth again, I'll tell the mother that the little one's happy where she is." But this made her remember her own little boys down on the earth, who were probably asking after their mother now.

Suddenly they turned up a mountain with terraces and little white houses, exactly like something she had once seen in a picture. And if that wasn't her brother standing outside one of the houses—he who had been so poor and miserable on earth!

"Why, is that you, Kari?" said her brother. "This

is my house," he went on, "and now I'm not bothered
with either taxes or debts. I've got plenty of both
food and firing, thank goodness, and I've no need to
work myself to death to make both ends meet. When
you've seen the Almighty, you mustn't forget to look
in here."

Kari was quite touched, but once more she thought:
"Poor Peter! he'll be alone on earth, toiling and moiling
as before."

At last they reached the top of the mountain, and
here stood the Almighty's own house. It was much
larger than the great cathedral she had seen once
when she was in the town. The Almighty, in bishop's
robes, was just going in, but stood still on seeing her.

Kari began to tremble, for she had heard that the
Almighty was very severe, and she knew that she had
many a time been different from what she should have
been so she stood still with downcast eyes and folded
hands.

"Ah, good day, Kari!" She heard to her astonishment that it was the Almighty himself who was speaking so gently to her. "Welcome to heaven! Come
and shake hands with me as our custom is."

Kari went timidly up to him, and falling on her
knees, began to cry, for she thought this was so much
too good for a poor sinner like herself.

"Rise, my child," said the Almighty, and he dried
her tears and told her that she must be happy now, for
all her sorrows would be turned into joy and happiness
here in heaven.

At this Kari found courage to say: "You musn't
for all the world think that I've had a hard time before

either. It's only bad people who say that Peter beat me, and I can't recollect that he ever took so much as a drop of spirits when he was in town. He was so good and kind to me, and we lived so happily together, that I don't remember that there was ever so much as a bad word between us."

"It's quite right and proper for you to speak so well of your husband," said the Almighty. "But now you must go with the angel there, and look about you in Paradise, and then decide what you want to do, and what you want to be here; for it is the custom here for everyone to be what he or she likes best."

"Oh," thought Kari, "it can't be very much that I'm good for"; but the angel who had fetched her, now took her with him, and they descended the mountain, but on the other side. They crossed little lakes, that shone rosy in the light of heaven, and on which swam flocks of white swans, singing more beautifully than she had ever heard anything sing before. The angel told her that these swans had also been people on earth, and that they had all had a talent for singing, but no money to pay for their training; so the Almighty had made them into swans, so that they could sing as beautifully as they liked. Along the banks Kari saw a great many water lilies rocking on the waves, with their open chalices turned toward the sky. The angel told her that these had been women who had been especially poetically inclined, but had never become what they meant to be on earth, and so the Almighty had blessed them in this way. The butterflies that fluttered about them were the Almighty's thoughts that now and then alighted and rested for a time on their petals.

The angel then asked Kari whether she would like to be either a swan or a water lily.

"Gracious, no!" she said, for she was thinking once more of Peter; and supposing he came here some day, it was not at all certain he would know her again if she were a water lily.

The angel showed her other lakes on which white and red boats were sailing about with gaily-dressed people on board playing on musical instruments. And she saw a large garden in which young men and women were dancing and gazing at one another with enamored glances. They were couples who had been separated on earth, and came together here; and the girls who had been plain and deformed on earth were the most beautiful of all here, so that they never sat out a single dance.

The angel asked Kari whether she would like to pass her time on board one of the boats, or become young and beautiful among those who danced. But Kari did not wish for either. And now too she remembered that the hay harvest would be going on down at Aasen, and how would Peter ever be able to get in the hay all alone!

Then Kari saw a great festival, where people sat eating and drinking at a richly spread table. Most of them had roses in their hair and were dressed in silk and velvet, and they leaned over to one another and drank toasts, and laughed so that they could be heard a long way off. The angel said that many of them had been poor on earth, and that a feast such as this had been their greatest wish, and so they were now having what they wanted. Then Kari saw another garden, in which slender women were walking with knights in narrow, grassy paths, each couple hidden from the others by trees and bushes, and it was thus they would have it.

The angel showed Kari a large gathering of men and women who were discussing complicated questions, adopting resolutions, and voting one another to the position of chairman; and he said that this was what these people had most desired on earth, and so they were allowed to amuse themselves in this way through all eternity. They looked exceedingly happy too, for their faces shone like little suns.

Kari shook her head, however, saying that this was a thing she had never understood.

Finally the angel showed her a garden in which a number of women were occupied in looking after little children. The angel said that some of these women had lost their children in life, but had found them again here, while others had longed for a child in life, but had never had one, generally because they had not married; but here they had the children of which they had dreamed, and nursed them, and put them to sleep, and washed and dressed them, and had never dreamt there could be such happiness even in heaven.

Kari thought, however, that when her own little boys were motherless on earth she could not bring herself to take charge of other people's children here.

When at last the angel brought her back to the Almighty, he was obliged to say that Kari could not make up her mind to anything.

"What!" exclaimed the Almighty. "Is there nothing in the whole kingdom of heaven that you think good enough?"

Kari fell upon her knees and burst into tears. "Oh,

it's not that, for everything is too good for me; but—but—" and she could get no farther.

"Don't be afraid to say what you want, for here everyone receives what he most desires."

These words encouraged Kari, and she said: "If that is the case, then I should like most of all to go back to earth again; for I can't see how Peter's going to manage alone."

All the angels standing round looked in alarm at the Almighty, for they had never yet heard of anyone wishing to give up Paradise in order to return to earth. But the Almighty only smiled, and said: "Would you like me to have your husband brought here at once?"

"My very humble thanks," said Kari, "but then Christian and Simon would be left without both father and mother."

"Yes, I've still got something for your boys to do on earth," said the Almighty. "But what is it you want, then!"

"Couldn't I go back to Aasen?" asked Kari timidly.

"I suppose I must let you then," said the Almighty. "But your body's already buried, so you'll always be invisible; and there's not much that you'll be able to do either."

"I would go with Peter wherever he goes, and with the boys where they go," said Kari. "If I could do that I should be just as happy as the angels here in Paradise."

"Well, I suppose I must let you then," said the Almighty good-naturedly. And he patted her on the head, and told the angel to take her back to earth again.

When they had gone so far down through the clouds that she could see Aasen, Kari was quite beside herself with joy. She recognized the cottage and the cowshed

and the fence a long way off. Smoke was rising from
the chimney, so they must have been cooking. The
angel now took leave of her, as she could easily find
her way alone.

When Kari came nearer, she saw that it was early
morning, for the meadows were covered with dew, and
people were trooping across the fields with scythe and
rake on their shoulders. Peter came out of the cowshed, leading the red-flanked cow which he was going
to tether, and then he carried in the milk. Poor fellow, he'd done the milking himself to-day, and that
was work he was not much accustomed to.

Kari perceived that he neither saw nor heard her,
but she followed him into the kitchen, seated herself
on the hearthstone, and watched him strain milk. It
was done carelessly, and not as it should have been
done. The strainer, she saw, had not been washed,
he spilled much of the milk on the floor when he
emptied the pail, and the milk pan was not clean either.
Didn't he know, the idiot, that in that way his milk
would soon go sour?

She then followed him into the bedroom when he
went to wake the boys and help them with their clothes.
Simon, the youngest, asked whether Mother had come
home, and his father told him he must leave off forever asking questions—Mother would come as soon
as she could. Kari patted both Simon and Christian on
the cheek, but neither of them seemed to notice it,
tho Christian looked several times straight toward
where she stood.

From that time, an entirely new life began for Kari
at Aasen. When the boys went to the forest to fetch
wood, she went with them to guard them from evil.

When Peter was taking in the hay on hot days, she
followed him and tried to make his burden lighter.
At night she remained beside his bed and the boys' to
see that they had no bad dreams. When Peter rose on
Sunday mornings, she tried to steal into his thoughts
and make him decide to go to church. She went into
the cowshed once every day to protect the cows from
disease; and in the autumn, when frosty nights came,
she went about the fields and persuaded the frost not
to touch Peter's corn.

Toward the end of the winter, Peter made up his
mind to take a trip into town, and now Kari did not
know what to do. Should she go with him, or should
she stay at home with the boys? It ended with her
staying at home, and while the boys tried to cook
their own food and to see to the cows in the cowshed,
she went about with them trying to show them how
to do it.

When Peter came home he was drunk, and beat the
boys just as he had so often beaten her; but the next
day he was remorseful as he always had been and
because, thank goodness, his conscience was not ruined
yet.

One day a strange woman came to the house with a
bundle under her arm, made herself at home and
took over the work in the kitchen and the cowshed.
A little while later, Kari saw that Peter was thinking
of getting married again. "Poor old fellow!" she
thought. "Is he really going to throw himself away
to another woman?" She had to look on while her
dresses and linen were used by the stranger. Later
in the spring, preparations for the wedding were made,

and one day the neighbors appeared with baskets on their arms, and drank to the happy couple.

The boys went about looking bashfully at one another, for they were thinking of their mother. Kari went with the little wedding party to the church, and sat far back in the choir, and watched Peter being wedded to another woman.

"It's too bad!" thought Kari. "She hasn't even tied his silk neckerchief properly round his neck. It usen't to be like that when I did it."

Things were very different for Peter now. He and his new wife frequently fought, and the boys were so ill treated by their stepmother that they often cried themselves to sleep.

The Almighty had seen all this, however, and one day an angel came flying down to Kari, and asked her if she would go with him to Paradise.

"Oh, no!" said Kari. "I don't think I should have a day's happiness there either, so long as things go with Peter as they're going now." So she stayed on, and was comforted in knowing that Peter thought of her more and more, and talked about her to the boys when the woman was not present.

Years passed, and the boys grew up and took places in the parish. They got on, and one of them married a farmer's daughter, who inherited both farm and land, and the other took a girl with money, and bought a boat and nets, and began fishing on a large scale.

A day came when Peter lay ill in the bed in which Kari had closed her eyes, and she sat on the edge of the bed, and passed her hand over his eyes in the hope that he would see her. At last he looked up and gazed at her.

"Oh, is that you, Kari?" he said.

"Yes, thank God, it's me," said Kari. "And I think we shall soon live together again."

"I expect you are pretty angry with me because I took another woman into the house," said Peter sadly.

"May the Almighty be as sure to forgive you as I am," said Kari, as she wiped his brow.

"He doesn't know what he's saying," said the woman, who was fidgeting about the room. "I'd better send for the priest."

At last Peter was free to go, and outside the door stood an angel, waiting to take them both to Paradise.

As before, the Almighty bade them welcome, and told them to look about them and decide what they would like to be.

An angel took them about and showed them all the splendors that were to be seen; and when at last they went back, the Almighty said: "Well, Peter Aasen, what have you decided for yourself and wife?"

Peter, who now knew that he might be exactly what he most wished to be, answered a little hesitatingly: "If you had a little piece of land that we could begin on, as we did when we were newly married, it would be more than we have deserved."

At this the Almighty laughed, and said to an angel: "Go with them to the great clearing, give them tools and timber for a cottage, and as much land as they want." And the angel took them to quite another part of Paradise, where Peter saw the finest land he had ever seen; and here the angel asked how much they wanted.

Kari and Peter looked at one another. "Well," said Peter, "on earth we had three cows, but now we can do with two."

The angel then gave them so much land that they would soon be able to feed two cows, and afterward, he said, they could add as much new land as they liked. At this Kari and Peter looked at one another, and thought they had never been so well off.

And then they began to work, as they had done when they were newly married. Peter dug, and Kari pulled up roots and made the ground even with the fork; and now and again they straightened their backs, wiped the perspiration from their brows, looked at one another, and laughed. As when they had first married. Peter was so industrious that he would not even have an afternoon nap; but Kari, as in their young days, would go out to him in the field, with his afternoon coffee in a little tin can. When they began to build the cottage, they decided that it should be exactly like the one at Aasen; that would be so nice when their sons came. And when at last they had a roof over their heads, and lay once more in their comfortable wide bed, they both agreed that no one in all Paradise could be so happy as they two.

THE MAN WITHOUT A COUNTRY

By EDWARD EVERETT HALE

I suppose that very few casual readers of the "New York Herald" of August 13, 1863, observed, in an obscure corner, among the "Deaths," the announcement:

"NOLAN. Died on board U. S. Corvette "Levant," Lat. 2° 11' S., Long. 131° W., on the 11th of May, PHILIP NOLAN."

I happened to observe it, because I was stranded at the old Mission House in Mackinaw, waiting for a Lake Superior steamer which did not choose to come, and I was devouring to the very stubble all the current literature I could get hold of, even down to the deaths and marriages in the "Herald." My memory for names and people is good, and the reader will see, as he goes on, that I had reason enough to remember Philip Nolan. There are hundreds of readers who would have paused at that announcement, if the officer of the "Levant" who reported it had chosen to make it thus: "Died, May 11, THE MAN WITHOUT A COUNTRY." For it was as "The Man Without a Country" that poor Philip Nolan had generally been known by the officers who had him in charge during some fifty years, as, indeed, by all the men who sailed under them. I dare say there is many a man who has taken wine with him once a fortnight, in a three years' cruise, who never knew that his name was "Nolan," or whether the poor wretch had any name at all.

There can now be no possible harm in telling this poor creature's story. Reason enough there has been till now, ever since Madison's administration went out in 1817, for very strict secrecy, the secrecy of honor itself, among the gentlemen of the navy who have had Nolan in successive charge. And certainly it speaks well for the *esprit de corps* of the profession, and the personal honor of its members, that to the press this man's story has been wholly unknown—and, I think, to the country at large also. I have reason to think, from some investigations I made in the Naval Archives when I was attached to the Bureau of Construction, that every official report relating to him was burned when Ross burned the public buildings at Washington. One of the Tuckers, or possibly one of the Watsons, had Nolan in charge at the end of the war; and when, on returning from his cruise, he reported at Washington to one of the Crowninshields—who was in the Navy Department when he came home—he found that the Department ignored the whole business. Whether they really knew nothing about it, or whether it was a *"Non mi ricordo,"* determined on as a piece of policy, I do not know. But this I do know, that since 1817, and possibly before, no naval officer had mentioned Nolan in his report.

But, as I say, there is no need for secrecy any longer. And now the poor creature is dead, it seems to me worth while to tell a little of his story, by way of showing young Americans of to-day what it is to be A MAN WITHOUT A COUNTRY.

．　．　．　．　．　．　．　．　．　．

Philip Nolan was as fine a young officer as there was in the "Legion of the West," as the Western division of our army was then called. When Aaron Burr made his first dashing expedition down to New Orleans in 1805, at Fort Massac, or somewhere above on the river, he met, as the Devil would have it, this gay, dashing, bright young fellow; at some dinner-party, I think. Burr marked him, talked to him, walked with him, took him a day or two's voyage in his flatboat, and, in short, fascinated him. For the next year, barrack-life was very tame to poor Nolan. He occasionally availed himself of the permission the great man had given him to write to him. Long, high-worded, stilted letters the poor boy wrote and rewrote and copied. But never a line did he have in reply from the gay deceiver. The other boys in the garrison sneered at him, because he sacrificed in this unrequited affection for a politician the time which they devoted to Monongahela, hazard, and high-lowjack. Bourbon, eucher, and poker were still unknown. But one day Nolan had his revenge. This time Burr came down the river not as an attorney seeking a place for his office, but as a disguised conqueror. He had defeated I know not how many district attorneys; he had dined at I know not how many public dinners; he had been heralded in I know not how many "Weekly Arguses," and it was rumored that he had an army behind him and an empire before him. It was a great day—his arrival—to poor Nolan. Burr had not been at the fort an hour before he sent for him. That evening he asked Nolan to take him out in his skiff, to show him a canebrake or a cotton-wood tree, as he said—really to seduce him; and by the time the sail was over, Nolan was enlisted body and soul. From that time, tho he did not yet know it, he lived as A MAN WITHOUT A COUNTRY.

What Burr meant to do I know no more than you,

dear reader. It is none of our business just now. Only, when the grand catastrophe came, and Jefferson and the House of Virginia of that day undertook to break on the wheel all the possible Clarences of the then House of York, by the great treason trial at Richmond, some of the lesser fry in that distant Mississippi Valley, which was further from us than Puget's Sound is to-day, introduced the like novelty on their provincial stage; and, to while away the monotony of the summer at Fort Adams, got up, for *spectacles,* a string of court-martials on the officers there. One and another of the colonels and majors were tried, and, to fill out the lost, little Nolan, against whom, Heaven knows, there was evidence enough— that he was sick of the service, had been willing to be false to it, and would have obeyed any order to march anywhither with any one who would follow him had the order been signed "by command of His Exc. A. Burr." The courts dragged on. The big flies escaped— rightly, for all I know. Nolan was proved guilty enough, as I say. Yet you and I would never have heard of him, reader, but that, when the president of the court asked him at the close whether he wished to say anything to show that he had always been faithful to the United States, he cried out in a fit of frenzy:

"Damn the United States! I wish I may never hear of the United States again!"

I suppose he did not know how the words shocked old Colonel Morgan, who was holding the court. Half the officers who sat in it had served through the Revolution, and their lives, not to say their necks, had been risked for the very idea which he so cavalierly cursed in his madness. He, on his part, had grown up in the

West of those days, in the midst of "Spanish plot," "Orleans plot," and all the rest. He had been educated on a plantation where the finest company was a Spanish officer or a French merchant from Orleans. His education, such as it was, had been perfected in commercial expeditions to Vera Cruz, and I think he told me his father once hired an Englishman to be a private tutor for a winter on the plantation. He had spent half his youth with an older brother, hunting horses in Texas, and, in a word, to him "United States" was scarcely a reality. Yet he had been fed by "United States" for all the years since he had been in the army. He had sworn on his faith as a Christian to be true to "United States." It was "United States" which gave him the uniform he wore, and the sword by his side. Nay, my poor Nolan, it was only because "United States" had picked you out first as one of her own confidential men of honor that "A. Burr" cared for you a straw more than for the flat-boat men who sailed his ark for him. I do not excuse Nolan; I only explain to the reader why he damned his country, and wished he might never hear her name again.

He heard her name but once again. From that moment, September 23, 1807, till the day he died, May 11, 1863, he never heard her name again. For that half-century and more he was a man without a country.

Old Morgan, as I said, was terribly shocked. If Nolan had compared George Washington to Benedict Arnold, or had cried "God save King George," Morgan would not have felt worse. He called the court into his private room, and returned in fifteen minutes, with a face like a sheet, to say:

"Prisoner, hear the sentence of the Court! The Court decides, subject to the approval of the President, that you never hear the name of the United States again."

Nolan laughed. But nobody else laughed. Old Morgan was too solemn, and the whole room was hushed dead as night for a minute. Even Nolan lost his swagger in a moment. Then Morgan added:

"Mr. Marshal, take the prisoner to Orleans in an armed boat, and deliver him to the naval commander there."

"Mr. Marshal," continued old Morgan, "see that no one mentions the United States to the prisoner. Mr. Marshal, make my respects to Lieutenant Mitchell at Orleans, and request him to order that no one shall mention United States to the prisoner while he is on board ship. You will receive your written orders from the officer on duty here this evening. The court is adjourned without day."

I have always supposed that Colonel Morgan himself took the proceedings of the court to Washington city and explained them to Mr. Jefferson. Certain it is that the President approved them—certain, that is, if I may believe the men who say they have seen his signature. Before the "Nautilus" got round from New Orleans to the northern Atlantic coast with the prisoner on board, the sentence had been approved, and he was a man without a country.

The plan then adopted was substantially the same which was necessarily followed ever after. Perhaps it was suggested by the necessity of sending him by water from Fort Adams and Orleans. The Secretary of the Navy—it must have been the first Crowninshield, tho he is a man I do not remember—was requested to put Nolan on board a government vessel bound on a long cruise, and to direct that he should be only so

far confined there as to make it certain that he never
saw or heard of the country. We had a few long
cruises then, and the navy was very much out of
favor; and as almost all of this story is traditional, as
I have explained, I do not know certainly what his
first cruise was. But the commander to whom he was
entrusted—perhaps it was Tingey or Shaw, tho I
think it was one of the younger men (we are all old
enough now)—regulated the etiquet and the precautions of the affair, and according to his scheme they
were carried out, I suppose, till Nolan died.

When I was second officer of the "Intrepid," some
thirty years after, I saw the original paper of instructions. I have been sorry ever since that I did not copy
the whole of it. It ran, however, much in this way:

"WASHINGTON (*with a date which
must have been late in 1807*).

"*Sir—You will receive from Lieutenant Neale the
person of Philip Nolan, late a lieutenant in the United
States Army.*

"*This person on his trial by court-martial exprest,
with an oath, the wish that he might 'never hear of the
United States again.'*

"*The Court sentenced him to have his wish fulfilled.*

"*For the present, the execution of the order is entrusted by the President to this Department.*

"*You will take the prisoner on board your ship, and
keep him there with such precautions as shall prevent
his escape.*

"*You will provide him with such quarters, rations,
and clothing as would be proper for an officer of his
late rank if he were a passenger on your vessel on the
business of his Government.*

"The gentlemen on board will make any arrangements agreeable to themselves regarding his society. He is to be exposed to no indignity of any kind, nor is he ever unnecessarily to be reminded that he is a prisoner.

"But under no circumstances is he ever to hear of his country or to see any information regarding it; and you will especially caution all the officers under your command to take care that, in the various indulgences which may be granted, this rule, in which his punishment is involved, shall not be broken.

"It is the intention of the Government that he shall never again see the country which he has disowned. Before the end of your cruise you will receive orders which will give effect to this intention.

> *"Respectfully yours,*
> *"W. Southard, for the*
> *"Secretary of the Navy.*

If I had only preserved the whole of this paper, there would be no break in the beginning of my sketch of this story. For Captain Shaw, if it were he, handed it to his successor in the charge, and he to his, and I suppose the commander of the "Levant" has it to-day.

The rule adopted on board the ships on which I have met "the man without a country" was, I think, transmitted from the beginning. No mess liked to have him permanently, because his presence cut off all talk of home or of the prospect of return, of politics or letters, of peace or of war—cut off more than half the talk men like to have at sea. But it was always thought too hard that he should never meet the rest of us, except to touch hats, and we finally sank into one system. He was not permitted to talk with the men unless an officer was by. With officers he had unstrained intercourse, as far as they and he chose. But he grew shy, tho he had favorites: I was one. Then the captain always asked him 'to dinner on Monday. Every mess in succession took up the invitation in its turn. According to the size of the ship, you had him at your mess more or less often at dinner. His breakfast he ate in his own stateroom—which was where a sentinel or somebody on the watch could see the door. And whatever else he ate or drank, he ate or drank alone. Sometimes, when the marines or sailors had any special jollification, they were permitted to invite "Plain-Buttons," as they called him. Then Nolan was sent with some officers, and the men were forbidden to speak of home while he was there. I believe the theory was that the sight of his punishment did them good. They called him "Plain-Buttons" because, while he always chose to wear a regulation army uniform, he was not permitted to wear the army button, for the reason that it bore either the initials or the insignia of the country he had disowned.

I remember, soon after I joined the navy, I was on shore with some of the older officers from our ship and from the "Brandywine," which we had met at Alexandria. We had leave to make a party and go up to Cairo and the Pyramids. As we jogged along (you went on donkeys then), some of the gentlemen (we boys called them "Dons," but the phrase was long since changed) fell to talking about Nolan, and some one told the system which was adopted from the first about his books and other reading. As he was almost never permitted to go on shore, even tho the vessel lay in port for months, his time at the best hung heavily;

and everybody was permitted to lend him books if
they were not published in America and made no
allusion to it. These were common enough in the old
days, when people in the other hemisphere talked of the
United States as little as we do of Paraguay. He had
almost all the foreign papers that came into the ship,
sooner or later; only somebody must go over them
first, and cut out any advertisement or stray paragraph
that alluded to America. This was a little cruel sometimes, when the back of what was cut out might be
as innocent as Hesiod. Right in the midst of one of
Napoleon's battles, or one of Canning's speeches, poor
Nolan would find a great hole, because on the back of
the page of that paper there had been an advertisement
of a packet for New York, or a scrap from the President's message. I say this was the first time I ever
heard of this plan, which afterward I had enough and
more than enough to do with. I remember it, because
poor Phillips, who was of the party, as soon as the
allusion to reading was made, told a story of something
which happened at the Cape of Good Hope on Nolan's
first voyage; and it is the only thing I ever knew of
that voyage. They had touched at the Cape, and had
done the civil thing with the English Admiral and the
fleet, and then, leaving for a long cruise up the Indian
Ocean, Phillips had borrowed a lot of English books
from an officer, which, in those days, as indeed in these,
was quite a windfall. Among them, as the Devil
would order, was the "Lay of the Last Minstrel,"
which they had all of them heard of, but which most
of them had never seen. I think it could not have been
published long. Well, nobody thought there could be
any risk of anything national in that, tho Phillips
swore old Shaw had cut out the "Tempest" from

Shakespeare before he let Nolan have it, because he said "the Bermudas ought to be ours, and, by Jove, should be one day." So Nolan was permitted to join the circle one afternoon when a lot of them sat on deck smoking and reading aloud. People do not do such things so often now, but when I was young we got rid of a great deal of time so. Well, so it happened that in his turn Nolan took the book and read to the others, and he read very well, as I know. Nobody in the circle knew a line of the poem, only it was all magic and Border chivalry, and was a thousand years old. Pool Nolan read steadily through the fifth canto, stopped a minute and drank something, and then began, without a thought of what was coming.

> "Breathes there the man, with soul so dead,
>   Who never to himself hath said"—

It seems impossible to us that anybody ever heard this for the first time; but all these fellows did then, and poor Nolan himself went on, still unconsciously or mechanically;

> "This is my own, my native land!"

Then they all saw something was to pay; but he expected to get through, I suppose, turned a little pale, but plunged on:

> "Whose heart hath ne'er within him burned,
>   As home his footsteps he hath turned
>   From wandering on a foreign strand?—
>   If such there breathe, go, mark him well"—

By this time the men were all beside themselves, wishing there was any way to make him turn over two

pages. But he had not quite presence of mind for that;
he gagged a little, colored crimson, and staggered on:

> "For him no minstrel raptures swell;
> High tho his titles, proud his name,
> Boundless his wealth as wish can claim,
> Despite these titles, power, and pelf,
> The wretch, concentred all in self"—

and here the poor fellow choked, could not go on,
but started up, swung the book into the sea, vanished
into his stateroom, "And, by Jove," said Phillips, "we
did not see him for two months again. And I had to
make up some beggarly story to that English surgeon
why I did not return his Walter Scott to him."

The story shows about the time when Nolan's
braggadocio must have broken down. At first, they
said, he took a very high tone, considered his imprisonment a mere farce, affected to enjoy the voyage, and
all that; but Phillips said that after he came out of his
stateroom he never was the same man again. He
never read aloud again, unless it was the Bible or
Shakespeare, or something else he was sure of. But
it was not that merely. He never entered in with the
other young men exactly as a companion again. He
was always shy afterward, when I knew him, very seldom spoke, unless he was spoken to, except to a very
few friends. He lighted up occasionally—I remember
late in his life hearing him fairly eloquent on something which had been suggested to him by one of
Fléchier's sermons—but generally he had the nervous,
tired look of a heart-wounded man.

When Captain Shaw was coming home—if, as I say,
it was Shaw—rather to the surprise of everybody they
made one of the Windward Islands, and lay off and on
for nearly a week. The boys said the officers were sick

of salt junk, and meant to have turtle soup before they came home. But after several days the "Warren" came to the same rendezvous; they exchanged signals, she sent to Phillips and these homeward-bound men letters and papers, and told them she was outward bound, perhaps to the Mediterranean, and took poor Nolan and his traps on the boat back to try his second cruise. He looked very blank when he was told to get ready to join her. He had known enough of the signs of the sky to know that till that moment he was going "home." But this was a distinct evidence of something he had not thought of, perhaps—that there was no going home for him, even to a prison.

It may have been on that second cruise—it was once when he was up the Mediterranean—that Mrs. Graff, the celebrated Southern beauty of those days, danced with him. They had been lying a long time in the Bay of Naples, and the officers were very intimate in the English fleet, and there had been great festivities, and our men thought they must give a great ball on board the ship. How they ever did it on board the "Warren" I am sure I do not know. Perhaps it was not the "Warren," or perhaps ladies did not take up so much room as they do now. They wanted to use Nolan's stateroom for something, and they hated to do it without asking him to the ball; so the captain said they might ask him if they would be responsible that he did not talk with the wrong people, "who would give him intelligence." So the dance went on, the finest party that had ever been known, I dare say; for I never heard of a man-of-war ball that was not. For ladies they had the family of the American consul, one or two travelers who had adven-

tured so far, and a nice bevy of English girls and ma-
trons, perhaps Lady Hamilton herself.

Well, different officers relieved each other in standing and talking with Nolan in a friendly way, so as to
be sure that nobody else spoke to him. The dancing
went on with spirit, and after a while even the fellows
who took this honorary guard of Nolan ceased to fear
any *contretemps*. Only when some English lady—
Lady Hamilton, as I said, perhaps—called for a set of
"American dances," an odd thing happened. Everybody then danced contra-dances. The black band,
nothing loath, conferred as to what "American dances"
were and started off with "Virginia Reel," which they
followed with "Money-Musk," which, in its turn in
those days, should have been followed by "The Old
Thirteen." But just as Dick, the leader, tapped for
his fiddles to begin, and bent forward, about to say,
in true negro state, " 'The Old Thirteen,' gentlemen
and ladies!" as he had said " 'Virginia Reel,' if you
please!" and " 'Money-Musk,' if you please!" the
captain's boy tapped him on the shoulder, whispered to
him, and he did not announce the name of the dance.
He merely bowed, began on the air, and they all fell
to—the officers teaching the English girls the figure,
but not telling them why it had no name.

But that is not the story I started to tell. As the
dancing went on, Nolan and our fellows all got at
ease, as I said—so much so, that it seemed quite natural for him to bow to that splendid Mrs. Graff, and
say:

"I hope you have not forgotten me, Miss Rutledge.
Shall I have the honor of dancing?"

He did it so quickly that Fellows, who was with him,
could not hinder him. She laughed and said: "I am

not Miss Rutledge any longer, Mr. Nolan, but I will dance all the same," just nodded to Fellows, as if to say he must leave Mr. Nolan to her, and led him off to the place where the dance was forming.

Nolan thought he had got his chance. He had known her at Philadelphia, and at other places had met her, and this was a godsend. You could not talk in contra-dances, as you do in cotillons, or even in the pauses of waltzing, but there were chances for tongues and sounds, as well as for eyes and blushes. He began with her travels, and Europe, and Vesuvius, and the French, and then, when they had worked down, and had that long talking time at the bottom of the set, he said boldly, a little pale, she said, as she told me the story years after:

"And what do you hear from home, Mrs. Graff?"

And that splendid creature looked through him. Jove! how she must have looked through him!

"Home!! Mr. Nolan!!! I thought you were the man who never wanted to hear of home again!" And she walked directly up the deck to her husband, and left poor Nolan alone, as he always was. He did not dance again.

These are the traditions, which I sort out, as I believe them, from the myths which have been told about the man for forty years. The lies that have been told about him are legion. The fellows used to say he was the "Iron Mask," and George Pons went to his grave in the belief that this was the author of "Junius," who was being punished for his celebrated libel on Thomas Jefferson. Pons was not very strong in the historical line.

A happier story than either of these I have told is of the war. That came along soon after. I have heard this affair told in three or four ways, and, indeed, it may have happened more than once. But which ship it was on I cannot tell. However, in one, at least, of the great frigate duels with the English, in which the navy was really baptized, it happened that a round shot from the enemy entered one of our ports square, and took right down the officer of the gun himself, and almost every man of the gun's crew. Now you may say what you choose about courage, but that is not a nice thing to see. But, as the men who were not killed picked themselves up, and as they and the surgeon's people were carrying off the bodies, there appeared Nolan, in his shirt-sleeves, with the rammer in his hand, and, just as if he had been the officer, told them off with authority—who should go to the cockpit with the wounded men, who should stay with him—perfectly cheery, and with that way which makes men feel sure all is right and is going to be right. And he finished loading the gun with his own hands, aimed it, and bade the men fire. And there he stayed, captain of that gun, keeping those fellows in spirits, till the enemy struck, sitting on the carriage while the gun was cooling, tho he was exposed all the time, showing them easier ways to handle heavy shot, making the raw hands laugh at their own blunders, and when the gun cooled again, getting it loaded and fired twice as often as any other gun on the ship. The captain walked forward by way of encouraging the men, and Nolan touched his hat and said:

"I am showing them how we do this in the artillery, sir."

And this is the part of the story where all the legends agree. The commodore said:

"I see you do, and I thank you, sir; and I shall never forget this day, sir, and you never shall, sir."

And after the whole thing was over, and he had the Englishman's sword, in the midst of the state and ceremony of the quarterdeck, he said:

"Where is Mr. Nolan? Ask Mr. Nolan to come here."

And when Nolan came, he said:

"Mr. Nolan, we are all very grateful to you to-day; you are one of us to-day; you will be named in the dispatches."

And then the old man took off his own sword of ceremony, and gave it to Nolan, and made him put it on. The man told me this who saw it. Nolan cried like a baby, and well he might. He had not worn a sword since that infernal day at Fort Adams. But always afterward, on occasions of ceremony, he wore that quaint old French sword of the commodore's.

The captain did mention him in the dispatches. It was always said he asked that he might be pardoned. He wrote a special letter to the Secretary of War. But nothing ever came of it.

I have heard it said that he was with Porter when he took possession of the Nukahiva Islands. Not this Porter, you know, but old Porter, his father, Essex Porter—that is, the old Essex Porter, not this Essex. As an artillery officer, who had seen service in the West, Nolan knew more about fortifications, embrasures, ravelins, stockades, and all that, than any of them did; and he worked with a right good will in fixing that battery all right. I have always thought it was a pity Porter did not leave him in command there with Gamble. That would have settled all the question about his punishment. We should have kept

the islands, and at this moment we should have one
station in the Pacific Ocean. Our French friends, too,
when they wanted this little watering-place, would
have found it was preoccupied. But Madison and the
Virginians, of course, flung all that away.

All that was near fifty years ago. If Nolan was
thirty then, he must have been near eighty when he
died. He looked sixty when he was forty. But he
never seemed to me to change a hair afterward. As I
imagine his life, from what I have seen and heard
of it, he must have been in every sea, and yet almost
never on land. He must have known, in a formal way,
more officers in our service than any man living
knows. He told me once, with a grave smile, that
no man in the world lived so methodical a life as he.
"You know the boys say I am the Iron Mask, and you
know how busy he was." He said it did not do for
any one to try to read all the time, more than to do
anything else all the time, but that he read just five
hours a day. "Then," he said, "I keep up my note-
books, writing in them at such and such hours from
which I have been reading, and I include in these my
scrap-books." These were very curious indeed. He
had six or eight, of different subjects. There was one
of History, one of Natural Science, one which he called
"Odds and Ends." But they were not merely books
of extracts from newspapers. They had bits of plants
and ribbons, shells tied on, and carved scraps of bone
and wood, which he had taught the men to cut for him,
and they were beautifully illustrated. He drew ad-
mirably. He had some of the funniest drawings there,
and some of the most pathetic that I have ever seen
in my life.

Well, he said his readings and his notes were his profession, and that they took five hours and two hours respectively of each day. "Then," said he, "every man should have a diversion as well as a profession. My Natural History is my diversion." That took two hours a day more. The men used to bring him birds and fish, but on a long cruise he had to satisfy himself with centipedes and cockroaches and such small game. He was the only naturalist I ever met who knew anything about the habits of the house-fly and the mosquito. All those people can tell you whether they are *Lepidoptera* or *Steptoptera;* but as for telling you how you can get rid of them, or how they get away from you when you strike at them—why, Linnæus knew as little of that as John Foy, the idiot, did.

These nine hours made Nolan's regular daily "occupation." The rest of the time he talked or walked. Till he grew very old, he went aloft a great deal. He always kept up his exercise, and I never heard that he was ill. If any other man was ill, he was the kindest nurse in the world; and he knew more than half the surgeons do. Then, if anybody was sick or died, or if the captain wanted him to, on any other occasion, he was always ready to read prayers.

My own acquaintance with Philip Nolan began six or eight years after the English war, on my first voyage after I was appointed a midshipman. It was in the first days after our Slave-Trade treaty, while the Reigning House, which was still the House of Virginia, had still a sort of sentimentalism about the suppression of the horrors of the Middle Passage, and something was sometimes done that way. We were in the South Atlantic on that business. From the time I joined, I believe I thought Nolan was a sort of lay chaplain—a chaplain with a blue coat. I never asked about him. Everything in the ship was strange to me. I knew it was green to ask questions, and I suppose I thought there was a "Plain-Buttons" on every ship. We had him to dine in our mess once a week, and the caution was given that on that day nothing was to be said about home. But if they had told us not to say anything about the planet Mars or the Book of Deuteronomy, I should not have asked why; there were a great many things which seemed to me to have as little reason.

I first came to understand anything about "the man without a country" one day when we overhauled a dirty little schooner which had slaves on board. An officer was sent to take charge of her, and, after a few minutes, he sent back his boat to ask that some one might be sent him who could speak Portuguese. We were all looking over the rail when the message came, and we all wished we could interpret, when the captain asked who spoke Portuguese. But none of the officers did, and just as the captain was sending forward to ask if any of the people could, Nolan stepped out and said he should be glad to interpret, if the captain wished, as he understood the language. The captain thanked him, fitted out another boat with him, and in this boat it was my luck to go. When we got there it was such a scene as you seldom see, and never want to. Nastiness beyond account, and chaos run loose in the midst of the nastiness. There were not a great many of the negroes; but by way of making what there were understand that they were free, Vaughan had had their handcuffs and anklecuffs knocked off, and, for convenience' sake, was putting them upon the rascals of the schooner's crew. The negroes were, most of them, out of the hold, and swarming all round the dirty deck,

with a central throng surrounding Vaughan and addressing him in every dialect and *patois* of a dialect,
from the Zulu click up to the Parisian of Beledeljereed.

As we came on deck, Vaughan looked down from a
hogshead, on which he had mounted in desperation,
and said:

"For God's love, is there anybody who can make
these wretches understand something? The men gave
them rum, and that did not quiet them. I knocked
that big fellow down twice, and that did not soothe
him. And then I talked Choctaw to all of them together, and I'll be hanged if they understood that as
well as they understood the English."

Nolan said he could speak Portuguese, and one or
two fine-looking Kroomen were dragged out, who, as
it had been found already, had worked for the Portuguese on the coast at Fernando Po.

"Tell them they are free," said Vaughan. "And
tell them that these rascals are to be hanged as soon as
we can get rope enough."

Nolan "put that into Spanish"—that is, he explained
it in such Portuguese as the Kroomen could understand, and they in turn to such of the negroes as could
understand them. Then there was such a yell of delight, clinching of fists, leaping and dancing, kissing of
Nolan's feet, and a general rush made to the hogshead
by way of spontaneous worship of Vaughan, as the
deus ex machina of the occasion.

"Tell them," said Vaughan, well pleased, "that I
will take them all to Cape Palmas."

This did not answer so well. Cape Palmas was prac-
tically as far from the homes of most of them as New
Orleans or Rio Janeiro was—that is, they would be
eternally separated from home there. And their in-

terpreters, as we could understand, instantly said, *"Ah, non Palmas,"* and began to propose infinite other expedients in most voluble language. Vaughan was rather disappointed at this result of his liberality, and asked Nolan eagerly what they said. The drops stood on poor Nolan's white forehead, as he hushed the men down, and said:

"He says, 'Not Palmas.' He says, 'Take us home, take us to our own country, take us to our own house, take us to our own pickaninnies and our own women.' He says he has an old father and mother who will die if they do not see him. And this one says he left his people all sick, and paddled down to Fernando to beg the white doctor to come and help them, and that these devils caught them in the bay just in sight of home, and that he has never seen anybody from home since then. And this one says," choked out Nolan, "that he has not heard a word from his home in six months, while he has been locked up in that infernal barracoon."

Vaughan always said he grew gray himself while Nolan struggled through this interpretation. I, who did not understand anything of the passion involved in it, saw that the very elements were melting with fervent heat, and that something was to pay somewhere. Even the negroes stopped howling, as they saw Nolan's agony and Vaughan's almost equal agony of sympathy. As quick as he could get words, he said:

"Tell them yes, yes, yes; tell them they shall go to the Mountains of the Moon if they will. If I sail the schooner through the Great White Desert, they shall go home!"

And after some fashion Nolan said so. And then

they all fell to kissing him again, and wanted to rub his nose with theirs.

But he could not stand it long, and, getting Vaughan to say he might go back, he beckoned me down into our boat. As we lay back in the stern-sheets and the men gave way, he said to me: "Youngster, let that show you what it is to be without a family, without a home, and without a country. And if you are ever tempted to say a word or to do a thing that shall put a bar between you and your family, your home, and your country, pray God in His mercy to take you that instant home to His own heaven. Stick by your family, boy; forget you have a self, while you do everything for them. Think of your home, boy; write and send and talk about it. Let it be nearer and nearer to your thought the further you have to travel from it; and rush back to it when you are free, as that poor black slave is doing now. And for your country, boy," and the words rattled in his throat, "and for that flag," and he pointed to the ship, "never dream a dream but of serving her as she bids you, tho the service carry you through a thousand hells. No matter what happens to you, no matter who flatters you or who abuses you, never look at another flag, never let a night pass but you pray God to bless that flag. Remember, boy, that behind all these men you have to do with, behind officers, and government, and people even, there is the Country Herself, your Country, and that you belong to Her as you belong to your own mother. Stand by Her, boy, as you would stand by your mother, if those devils there had got hold of her to-day!"

I was frightened to death by his calm, hard passion, but I blundered out that I would, by all that was holy, and that I had never thought of doing anything else.

He hardly seemed to hear me, but he did, almost in a whisper, say: "Oh, if anybody had said so to me when I was of your age!"

I think it was this half-confidence of his, which I never abused, for I never told this story till now, which afterward made us great friends. He was very kind to me. Often he sat up, or even got up, at night, to walk the deck with me, when it was my watch. He explained to me a great deal of my mathematics, and I owe to him my taste for mathematics. He lent me books, and helped me about my reading. He never alluded so directly to his story again, but from one and another officer I have learned, in thirty years, what I am telling. When we parted from him in St. Thomas harbor at the end of our cruise I was more sorry than I can tell. I was very glad to meet him again in 1830; and later in life, when I thought I had some influence in Washington, I moved heaven and earth to have him discharged. But it was like getting a ghost out of prison. They pretended there was no such man, and never was such a man. They will say so at the Department now! Perhaps they do not know.

There is a story that Nolan met Burr once on one of our vessels, when a party of Americans came on board in the Mediterranean. But this I believe to be a lie; or, rather, it is a myth, *ben trovato,* involving a tremendous blowing-up with which he sunk Burr, asking how he liked to be "without a country." But it is clear from Burr's life that nothing of the sort could have happened, and I mention this only as an illustration of the stories which get a-going where there is the least mystery at bottom.

So poor Philip Nolan had his wish fulfilled. I know

but one fate more dreadful: it is the fate reserved for those men who shall have one day to exile themselves from their country because they have attempted her ruin, and shall have at the same time to see the prosperity and honor to which she rises when she has rid herself of them and their iniquities. The wish of poor Nolan, as we all learned to call him, not because his punishment was too great, but because his repentance was so clear, was precisely the wish of every Bragg and Beauregard who broke a soldier's oath two years ago, and of every Maury and Barron who broke a sailor's. I do not know how often they have repented. I do know that they have done all that in them lay that they might have no country, that all the honors, associations, memories, and hopes which belong to "country" might be broken up into little shreds and distributed to the winds. I know, too, that their punishment, as they vegetate through what is left of life to them in wretched Boulognes and Leicester Squares, where they are destined to upbraid each other till they die, will have all the agony of Nolan's, with the added pang that every one who sees them will see them to despise and to execrate them. They will have their wish, like him.

For him, poor fellow, he repented of his folly, and then, like a man, submitted to the fate he had asked for. He never intentionally added to the difficulty or delicacy of the charge of those who had him in hold. Accidents would happen, but they never happened from his fault. Lieutenant Truxton told me that, when Texas was annexed, there was a careful discussion among the officers, whether they should get hold of Nolan's handsome set of maps and cut Texas out of it—from the map of the world and the map of Mex-

ico. The United States had been cut out when the
atlas was bought for him. But it was voted, rightly
enough, that to do this would be virtually to reveal to
him what had happened, or, as Harry Cole said, to
make him think old Burr had succeeded. So it was
from no fault of Nolan's that a great botch happened
at my own table, when, for a short time, I was in command of the "George Washington" corvette, on the
South American station. We were lying in the La
Plata, and some of the officers, who had been on shore
and had just joined again, were entertaining us with
accounts of their misadventures in riding the half-wild
horses of Buenos Ayres. Nolan was at table, and was
in an unusually bright and talkative mood. Some
story of a tumble reminded him of an adventure of
his own when he was catching wild horses in Texas
with his adventurous cousin, at a time when he must
have been quite a boy. He told the story with a good
deal of spirit—so much so that the silence which often
follows a good story hung over the table for an instant, to be broken by Nolan himself. For he asked
perfectly unconsciously:

"Pray, what has become of Texas? After the Mex-
icans got their independence, I thought that province
of Texas would come forward very fast. It is really
one of the finest regions on earth; it is the Italy of
this continent. But I have not seen or heard a word
of Texas for near twenty years."

There were two Texas officers at the table. The
reason he had never heard of Texas was that Texas
and her affairs had been painfully cut out of his newspapers since Austin began his settlement, so that, while
he read of Honduras and Tamaulipas, and, till quite
lately, of California, this virgin province, in which his

brother had traveled so far, and, I believe, had died, had ceased to be to him. Waters and Williams, the two Texas men, looked grimly at each other and tried not to laugh. Edward Morris had his attention attracted by the third link in the chain of the captain's chandelier. Watrous was seized with a convulsion of sneezing. Nolan himself saw that something was to pay, he did not know what. And I, as master of the feast, had to say:

"Texas is out of the map, Mr. Nolan. Have you seen Captain Back's curious account of Sir Thomas Roe's Welcome?"

After that cruise I never saw Nolan again. I wrote to him at least twice a year, for in that voyage we became even confidentially intimate; but he never wrote to me. The other men tell me that in those fifteen years he *aged* very fast, as well he might, indeed, but that he was still the same gentle, uncomplaining, silent sufferer that he ever was, bearing as best he could his self-appointed punishment—rather less social, perhaps, with new men whom he did not know, but more anxious, apparently, than ever to serve and befriend and teach the boys, some of whom fairly seemed to worship him. And now it seems the dear old fellow is dead. He has found a home at last, and a country.

Since writing this, and while considering whether or no I would print it, as a warning to the young Nolans and Vallandighams and Tatnalls of to-day, I have received from Danforth, who is on board the "Levant," a letter which gives an account of Nolan's last hours. It removes all my doubts about telling this story.

To understand the first words of the letter, the non-professional reader should remember that after 1817 the position of every officer who had Nolan in charge

was one of the greatest delicacy. The government had
failed to renew the order of 1807 regarding him. What
was a man to do? Should he let him go? What, then,
if he were called to account by the Department for
violating the order of 1807? Should he keep him?
What, then, if Nolan should be liberated some day, and
should bring an action for false imprisonment or kid-
napping against every man who had had him in charge?
I urged and pressed this upon Southard, and I have
reason to think that other officers did the same thing.
But the Secretary always said, as they so often do at
Washington, that there were no special orders to give,
and that we must act on our own judgment. That
means, "If you succeed, you will be sustained; if you
fail, you will be disavowed." Well, as Danforth says,
all that is over now, tho I do not know but I expose
myself to a criminal prosecution on the evidence of the
very revelation I am making.

Here is the letter:

"LEVANT, 2° 2' S. @ 131° W.

"*Dear Fred—I try to find heart and life to tell you
that it is all over with dear old Nolan. I have been
with him on this voyage more than I ever was, and I
can understand wholly now the way in which you used
to speak of the dear old fellow. I could see that he
was not strong, but I had no idea the end was so near.
The doctor has been watching him very carefully, and
yesterday morning came to me and told me that Nolan
was not so well, and had not left his stateroom—a
thing I never remember before. He had let the doctor
come and see him as he lay there—the first time the
doctor had been in the stateroom—and he said he
should like to see me. Oh, dear! do you remember*

the mysteries we boys used to invent about his room in the old 'Intrepid' days? Well, I went in, and there, to be sure, the poor fellow lay in his berth, smiling pleasantly as he gave me his hand, but looking very frail. I could not help a glance round, which showed me what a little shrine he had made of the box he was lying in. The Stars and Stripes were triced up above and around a picture of Washington, and he had painted a majestic eagle, with lightnings blazing from his beak and his foot just clasping the whole globe, which his wings overshadowed. The dear old boy saw my glance, and said, with a sad smile, 'Here, you see, I have a country!' And then he pointed to the foot of his bed, where I had not seen before a great map of the United States, as he had drawn it from memory, and which he had there to look upon as he lay. Quaint, queer old names were on it, in large letters: 'Indiana Territory,' 'Mississippi Territory,' and 'Louisiana Territory,' as I suppose our fathers learned such things. But the old fellow had patched in Texas, too; he had carried his western boundary all the way to the Pacific, but on that shore he had defined nothing.

"'Oh, Danforth,' he said, 'I know I am dying. I can not get home. Surely you will tell me something now? Stop! Stop! Do not speak till I say what I am sure you know, that there is not in this ship, that there is not in America—God bless her!—a more loyal man than I. There can not be a man who loves the old flag as I do, or prays for it as I do, or hopes for it as I do. There are thirty-four stars in it now, Danforth. I thank God for that, tho I do not know what their names are. There has never been one taken away; I thank God for that. I know by that that

*there has never been any successful Burr. Oh, Dan-
forth, Danforth,' he sighed out, 'how like a wretched
night's dream a boy's idea of personal fame or of
separate sovereignty seems, when one looks back on
it after such a life as mine! But tell me—tell me
something—tell me everything, Danforth, before I
die!'*

"Ingham, I swear to you that I felt like a monster
that I had not told him everything before. Danger or
no danger, delicacy or no delicacy, who was I, that I
should have been acting the tyrant all this time over
this dear, sainted old man, who had years ago expiated,
in his whole manhood's life, the madness of a boy's
treason? 'Mr. Nolan,' said I, 'I will tell you everything you ask about. Only, where shall I begin?'

"Oh, the blessed smile that crept over his white
face! And he pressed my hand and said, 'God bless
you! Tell me their names,' he said, and he pointed to
the stars on the flag. 'The last I know is Ohio. My
father lived in Kentucky. But I have guessed Michigan
and Indiana and Mississippi—that was where Fort
Adams is. They make twenty. But where are your
other fourteen? You have not cut up any of the old
ones, I hope?'

"Well, that was not a bad text, and I told him the
names in as good order as I could, and he bade me take
down his beautiful map and draw them in as I best
could with my pencil. He was wild with delight about
Texas—told me how his cousin died there; he had
marked a gold cross near where he supposed his grave
was; and he had guessed at Texas. Then he was de-
lighted as he saw California and Oregon. That, he
said, he had suspected partly, because he had never

been permitted to land on that shore, tho the ships were there so much. 'And the men,' said he, laughing, 'brought off a good deal besides furs.' Then he went back—heavens, how far!—to ask about the 'Chesapeake,' and what was done to Barron for surrendering her to the 'Leopard,' and whether Burr ever tried again —and he ground his teeth with the only passion he showed. But in a moment that was over, and he said, 'God forgive me, for I am sure I forgive him.' Then he asked about the old war—told me the true story of his serving the gun the day we took the 'Java'—asked about dear old David Porter, as he called him. Then he settled down more quietly, and very happily, to hear me tell in an hour the history of fifty years.

"How I wished it had been somebody who knew something! But I did as well as I could. I told him of the English war. I told him about Fulton and the steamboat beginning. I told him about old Scott, and Jackson—told him all I could think of about the Mississippi, and New Orleans, and Texas, and his own old Kentucky. And what do you think he asked? 'Who was in command of the Legion of the West!' I told him it was a very gallant officer named Grant, and that, by our last news, he was about to establish his headquarters at Vicksburg. Then, 'Where was Vicksburg?' I worked that out on the map; it was about a hundred miles, more or less, above his old Fort Adams, and I thought Fort Adams must be a ruin now. 'It must be at old Vick's plantation, at Walnut Hills,' said he; 'well, that is a change!'

"I tell you, Ingham, it was a hard thing to condense the history of half a century into that talk with a sick man. And I do not know what I told him—of emi-

gration, and the means of it—of steamboats, and railroads, and telegraphs—of inventions, and books, and literature—of the colleges, and West Point, and the Naval School—but with the queerest interruptions that ever you heard. You see, it was Robinson Crusoe asking all the accumulated questions of fifty-six years!

"I remember he asked, all of a sudden, who was President now. And when I told him, he asked if Old Abe was General Benjamin Lincoln's son. He said he met old General Lincoln, when he was quite a boy himself, at some Indian treaty. I said no, that Old Abe was a Kentuckian like himself, but I could not tell him of what family; he had worked up from the ranks. 'Good for him!' cried Nolan; 'I am glad of that. As I have brooded and wondered, I have thought our danger was in keeping up those regular successions in the first families.' Then I got talking about my visit to Washington. I told him of meeting the Oregon Congressman, Harding; I told him about the Smithsonian, and the exploring Expedition; I told him about the Capitol, and the statues for the pediment, and Crawford's Liberty, and Greenough's Washington. Ingham, I told him everything I could think of that would show the grandeur of his country and its prosperity; but I could not make up my mouth to tell him a word about this infernal rebellion.

"And he drank it in and enjoyed it as I can not tell you. He grew more and more silent, yet I never thought he was tired or faint. I gave him a glass of water, but he just wet his lips, and told me not to go away. Then he asked me to bring the Presbyterian 'Book of Public Prayer,' which lay there, and said, with a smile, that it would open at the right place—

and so it did. There was his double red mark down the page. And I knelt down and read, and he repeated with me, 'For ourselves and our country, oh, gracious God, we thank Thee that, notwithstanding our manifold transgressions of Thy holy laws, Thou hast continued to us Thy marvelous kindness'—and so to the end of that thanksgiving. Then he turned to the end of the same book, and I read the words more familiar to me: 'Most heartily we beseech Thee with Thy favor to behold and bless Thy servant, the President of the United States, and all others in authority'—and the rest of the Episcopal collect. 'Danforth,' said he, 'I have repeated those prayers night and morning, it is now fifty-five years.' And then he said he would go to sleep.

"He bent me down over him and kissed me, and he said, 'Look in my Bible, Danforth, when I am gone.' And I went away.

"But I had no thought it was the end. I thought he was tired and would sleep. I knew he was happy, and I wanted him to be alone.

"But in an hour, when the doctor went in gently, he found Nolan had breathed his life away with a smile. He had something pressed close to his lips. It was his father's badge of the Order of the Cincinnati.

"We looked in his Bible, and there was a slip of paper at the place where he had marked the text:

"'They desire a country, even a heavenly: wherefore God is not ashamed to be called their God: for He hath prepared for them a city.'

"On this slip of paper he had written:

"'Bury me in the sea; it has been my home, and I love it. But will not some one set up a stone for my

memory at Fort Adams or at Orleans, that my disgrace
may not be more than I ought to bear? Say on it:

> "'In Memory of

> "'PHILIP NOLAN,

> "'Lieutenant in the Army of the United States.
> "'He loved his country as no other man has
> loved her; but no man deserved
> less at her hands.'"

A SOURCE OF IRRITATION

By Stacy Aumonier

To look at old Sam Gates you would never suspect him of having nerves. His sixty-nine years of close application to the needs of the soil had given him a certain earthy stolidity. To observe him hoeing, or thinning out a broad field of turnips, hardly attracted one's attention, he seemed so much part and parcel of the whole scheme. He blended into the soil like a glorified swede. Nevertheless, the half-dozen people who claimed his acquaintance knew him to be a man who suffered from little moods of irritability.

And on this glorious morning a little incident annoyed him unreasonably. It concerned his niece Aggie. She was a plump girl with clear, blue eyes, and a face as round and inexpressive as the dumplings for which the county was famous. She came slowly across the long sweep of the downland and, putting down the bundle wrapped in a red handkerchief which contained his breakfast and dinner, she said:

"Well, Uncle, is there any noos?"

Now, this may not appear to the casual reader to be a remark likely to cause irritation, but it affected old Sam Gates as a very silly and unnecessary question. It was, moreover, the constant repetition of it which was beginning to anger him. He met his niece twice a day. In the morning she brought his bundle of food at seven, and when he passed his sister's cottage on the way home to tea at five she was invariably hanging about the gate, and she always said in the same voice:

"Well, Uncle, is there any noos?"

Noos! What noos should there be? For sixty-nine years he had never lived farther than five miles from Halvesham. For nearly sixty of those years he had bent his back above the soil. There were, indeed, historic occasions. Once, for instance, when he had married Annie Hachet. And there was the birth of his daughter. There was also a famous occasion when he had visited London. Once he had been to a flower-show at Market Roughborough. He either went or didn't go to church on Sundays. He had had many interesting chats with Mr. James at the Cowman, and three years ago had sold a pig to Mrs. Way. But he couldn't always have interesting noos of this sort up his sleeve. Didn't the silly zany know that for the last three weeks he had been hoeing and thinning out turnips for Mr. Hodge on this very same field? What noos could there be?

He blinked at his niece, and didn't answer. She undid the parcel and said:

"Mrs. Goping's fowl got out again last night."

"Ah," he replied in a noncommittal manner and began to munch his bread and bacon. His niece picked up the handkerchief and, humming to herself, walked back across the field.

It was a glorious morning, and a white sea mist added to the promise of a hot day. He sat there munching, thinking of nothing in particular, but gradually subsiding into a mood of placid content. He no-

ticed the back of Aggie disappear in the distance.
It was a mile to the cottage and a mile and a half
to Halvesham. Silly things, girls. They were all
alike. One had to make allowances. He dismissed
her from his thoughts, and took a long swig of tea
out of a bottle. Insects buzzed lazily. He tapped
his pocket to assure himself that his pouch of shag
was there, and then he continued munching. When
he had finished, he lighted his pipe and stretched
himself comfortably. He looked along the line of
turnips he had thinned and then across the adjoining field of swedes. Silver streaks appeared on the
sea below the mist. In some dim way he felt happy
in his solitude amidst this sweeping immensity of
earth and sea and sky.

And then something else came to irritate him: it
was one of "these dratted airyplanes." "Airyplanes"
were his pet aversion. He could find nothing to be
said in their favor. Nasty, noisy, disfiguring things
that seared the heavens and made the earth dangerous. And every day there seemed to be more and
more of them. Of course "this old war" was responsible for a lot of them, he knew. The war
was a "plaguy noosance." They were short-handed
on the farm, beer and tobacco were dear, and Mrs. Ste-
ven's nephew had been and got wounded in the foot.

He turned his attention once more to the turnips;
but an "airyplane" has an annoying genius for grip-
ping one's attention. When it appears on the scene,
however much we dislike it, it has a way of taking
the stage-center. We cannot help constantly looking
at it. And so it was with old Sam Gates. He spat
on his hands and blinked up at the sky. And suddenly the aeroplane behaved in a very extraordinary

manner. It was well over the sea when it seemed to lurch drunkenly and skimmed the water. Then it shot up at a dangerous angle and zigzagged. It started to go farther out, and then turned and made for the land. The engines were making a curious grating noise. It rose once more, and then suddenly dived downward, and came plump down right in the middle of Mr. Hodge's field of swedes.

And then, as if not content with this desecration, it ran along the ground, ripping and tearing twenty-five yards of good swedes, and then came to a stop.

Old Sam Gates was in a terrible state. The aeroplane was more than a hundred yards away, but he waved his arms and called out:

"Hi, you there, you musn't land in they swedes! They're Mister Hodge's."

The instant the aeroplane stopped, a man leaped out and gazed quickly round. He glanced at Sam Gates, and seemed uncertain whether to address him or whether to concentrate his attention on the flying-machine. The latter arrangement appeared to be his ultimate decision. He dived under the engine and became frantically busy. Sam had never seen any one work with such furious energy; but all the same it was not to be tolerated. It was disgraceful. Sam started out across the field, almost hurrying in his indignation. When he appeared within earshot of the aviator he cried out again:

"Hi! you mustn't rest your old airyplane here! You've kicked up all Mr. Hodge's swedes. A noice thing you've done!"

He was within five yards when suddenly the aviator turned and covered him with a revolver! And speaking in a sharp, staccato voice, he said:

"Old Grandfather, you must sit down. I am very much occupied. If you interfere or attempt to go away, I shoot you. So!"

Sam gazed at the horrid, glittering little barrel and gasped. Well, he never! To be threatened with murder when you're doing your duty in your employer's private property! But, still, perhaps the man was mad. A man must be more or less mad to go up in one of those crazy things. And life was very sweet on that summer morning despite sixty-nine years. He sat down among the swedes.

The aviator was so busy with his cranks and machinery that he hardly deigned to pay him any attention except to keep the revolver handy. He worked feverishly, and Sam sat watching him. At the end of ten minutes he appeared to have solved his troubles with the machine, but he still seemed very scared. He kept on glancing round and out to sea. When his repairs were complete he straightened his back and wiped the perspiration from his brow. He was apparently on the point of springing back into the machine and going off when a sudden mood of facetiousness, caused by relief from the strain he had endured, came to him. He turned to old Sam and smiled, at the same time remarking:

"Well, old Grandfather, and now we shall be all right, isn't it?"

He came close up to Sam, and suddenly started back.

"Gott!" he cried, "Paul Jouperts!"

Bewildered, Sam gazed at him, and the madman started talking to him in some foreign tongue. Sam shook his head.

"You no roight," he remarked, "to come bargin' through they swedes of Mr. Hodge's."

And then the aviator behaved in a most peculiar manner. He came up and examined Sam's face very closely, and gave a sudden tug at his beard and hair, as if to see whether they were real or false.

"What is your name, old man?" he said.

"Sam Gates."

The aviator muttered some words that sounded something like "mare vudish," and then turned to his machine. He appeared to be dazed and in a great state of doubt. He fumbled with some cranks, but kept glancing at old Sam. At last he got into the car and strapped himself in. Then he stopped, and sat there deep in thought. At last he suddenly unstrapped himself and sprang out again and, approaching Sam, said very deliberately:

"Old Grandfather, I shall require you to accompany me."

Sam gasped.

"Eh?" he said. "What be talkin' about? 'Company? I got these 'ere loines o' turnips—I be already behoind—"

The disgusting little revolver once more flashed before his eyes.

"There must be no discussion," came the voice. "It is necessary that you mount the seat of the car without delay. Otherwise I shoot you like the dog you are. So!"

Old Sam was hale and hearty. He had no desire to die so ignominiously. The pleasant smell of the Norfolk downland was in his nostrils; his foot was on his native heath. He mounted the seat of the car, contenting himself with a mutter:

"Well, that be a noice thing, I must say! Flyin'
about the country with all they turnips on'y half
thinned!"

He found himself strapped in. The aviator was
in a fever of anxiety to get away. The engines made
a ghastly splutter and noise. The thing started running along the ground. Suddenly it shot upward,
giving the swedes a last contemptuous kick. At
twenty minutes to eight that morning old Sam found
himself being borne right up above his fields and
out to sea! His breath came quickly. He was a
little frightened.

"God forgive me!" he murmured.

The thing was so fantastic and sudden that his
mind could not grasp it. He only felt in some vague
way that he was going to die, and he struggled to
attune his mind to the change. He offered up a
mild prayer to God, Who, he felt, must be very near,
somewhere up in these clouds. Automatically he
thought of the vicar at Halvesham, and a certain
sense of comfort came to him at the reflection that
on the previous day he had taken a "cooking of
runner beans" to God's representative in that village.
He felt calmer after that, but the horrid machine
seemed to go higher and higher. He could not turn
in his seat and he could see nothing but sea and sky.
Of course the man was mad, mad as a March hare.
Of what earthly use could *he* be to any one? Besides, he had talked pure gibberish, and called him
Paul something, when he had already told him that
his name was Sam. The thing would fall down into
the sea soon, and they would both be drowned. Well,
well, he had almost reached three-score years and
ten. He was protected by a screen, but it seemed

very cold. What on earth would Mr. Hodge say?
There was no one left to work the land but a fool
of a boy named Billy Whitehead at Dene's Cross.
On, on, on they went at a furious pace. His thoughts
danced disconnectedly from incidents of his youth,
conversations with the vicar, hearty meals in the open,
a frock his sister wore on the day of the postman's
wedding, the drone of a psalm, the illness of some
ewes belonging to Mr. Hodge. Everything seemed
to be moving very rapidly, upsetting his sense of
time. He felt outraged, and yet at moments there
was something entrancing in the wild experience. He
seemed to be living at an incredible pace. Perhaps
he was really dead and on his way to the kingdom
of God. Perhaps this was the way they took people.

After some indefinite period he suddenly caught
sight of a long strip of land. Was this a foreign
country, or were they returning? He had by this
time lost all feeling of fear. He became interested
and almost disappointed. The "airyplane" was not
such a fool as it looked. It was very wonderful to
be right up in the sky like this. His dreams were
suddenly disturbed by a fearful noise. He thought
the machine was blown to pieces. It dived and ducked
through the air, and things were bursting all round
it and making an awful din, and then it went up
higher and higher. After a while these noises ceased,
and he felt the machine gliding downward. They
were really right above solid land—trees, fields, streams
and white villages. Down, down, down they glided.
This was a foreign country. There were straight
avenues of poplars and canals. This was not Halvesham. He felt the thing glide gently and bump
into a field. Some men ran forward and approached

them, and the mad aviator called out to them. They
were mostly fat men in gray uniforms, and they all
spoke this foreign gibberish. Some one came and
unstrapped him. He was very stiff and could hardly
move. An exceptionally gross-looking man punched
him in the ribs and roared with laughter. They all
stood round and laughed at him, while the mad aviator talked to them and kept pointing at him. Then
he said:

"Old Grandfather, you must come with me."

He was led to an iron-roofed building and shut in
a little room. There were guards outside with fixed
bayonets. After a while the mad aviator appeared
again, accompanied by two soldiers. He beckoned
him to follow. They marched through a quadrangle
and entered another building. They went straight
into an office where a very important-looking man,
covered with medals, sat in an easy-chair. There
was a lot of saluting and clicking of heels. The
aviator pointed at Sam and said something, and the
man with the medals started at sight of him, and
then came up and spoke to him in English.

"What is your name? Where do you come from?
Your age? The name and birthplace of your parents?

He seemed intensely interested, and also pulled his
hair and beard to see if they came off. So well and
naturally did he and the aviator speak English that
after a voluble examination they drew apart, and
continued the conversation in that language. And the
extraordinary conversation was of this nature:

"It is a most remarkable resemblance," said the
man with medals. *"Unglaublich!* But what do you
want me to do with him, Hausemann?"

"The idea came to me suddenly, Excellency," replied the aviator, "and you may consider it worth-

less. It is just this. The resemblance is so amazing.
Paul Jouperts has given us more valuable information than any one at present in our service, and the
English know that. There is an award of five thousand francs on his head. Twice they have captured
him, and each time he escaped. All the company
commanders and their staff have his photograph.
He is a serious thorn in their flesh."

"Well?" replied the man with the medals.

The aviator whispered confidentially:

"Suppose, your Excellency, that they found the
dead body of Paul Jouperts?"

"Well?" replied the big man.

"My suggestion is this. Tomorrow, as you know,
the English are attacking Hill 701, which for tactical
reasons we have decided to evacuate. If after the
attack they find the dead body of Paul Jouperts in,
say, the second lines, they will take no further trouble
in the matter. You know their lack of thorough-
ness. Pardon me, I was two years at Oxford Uni-
versity. And consequently Paul Jouperts will be able
to prosecute his labors undisturbed."

The man with the medals twirled his mustache
and looked thoughtfully at his colleague.

"Where is Paul at the moment?" he asked.

"He is acting as a gardener at the Convent of
St. Eloise, at Mailleton-enhaut, which, as you know,
is one hundred meters from the headquarters of the
British central army staff."

The man with the medals took two or three rapid
turns up and down the room, then he said:

"Your plan is excellent, Hausemann. The only
point of difficulty is that the attack started this
morning."

"This morning?" exclaimed the other.

"Yes; the English attacked unexpectedly at dawn. We have already evacuated the first line. We shall evacuate the second line at eleven-fifty. It is now ten-fifteen. There may be just time."

He looked suddenly at old Sam in the way that a butcher might look at a prize heifer at an agricultural show and remarked casually:

"Yes, it is a remarkable resemblance. It seems a pity not to—do something with it."

Then, speaking in German, he added:

"It is worth trying. And if it succeeds, the higher authorities shall hear of your lucky accident and inspiration, Herr Hausemann. Instruct *Ober-lieutenant* Schultz to send the old fool by two orderlies to the east extremity of Trench 38. Keep him there till the order of evacuation is given, then shoot him, but don't disfigure him, and lay him out face upward."

The aviator saluted and withdrew, accompanied by his victim. Old Sam had not understood the latter part of the conversation, and he did not catch quite all that was said in English; but he felt that somehow things were not becoming too promising, and it was time to assert himself. So he remarked when they got outside:

"Now, look 'ee 'ere, Mister, when am I goin' to get back to my turnips?"

And the aviator replied, with a pleasant smile:

"Do not be disturbed, old Grandfather. You shall get back to the soil quite soon."

In a few moments he found himself in a large gray car, accompanied by four soldiers. The aviator left him. The country was barren and horrible, full of great pits and rents, and he could hear the roar of artillery and the shriek of shells. Overhead, aeroplanes were buzzing angrily. He seemed to be suddenly transported from the kingdom of God to the pit of darkness. He wondered whether the vicar had enjoyed the runner beans. He could not imagine runner beans growing here; runner beans, aye, or anything else. If this was a foreign country, give him dear old England!

Gr-r-r! bang! Something exploded just at the rear of the car. The soldiers ducked, and one of them pushed him in the stomach and swore.

"An ugly-looking lout," he thought. "If I wor twenty years younger, I'd give him a punch in the eye that 'u'd make him sit up."

The car came to a halt by a broken wall. The party hurried out and dived behind a mound. He was pulled down a kind of shaft, and found himself in a room buried right underground, where three officers were drinking and smoking. The soldiers saluted and handed them a typewritten dispatch. The officers looked at him drunkenly, and one came up and pulled his beard and spat in his face and called him "an old English swine." He then shouted out some instructions to the soldiers, and they led him out into the narrow trench. One walked behind him, and occasionally prodded him with the butt-end of a gun. The trenches were half full of water and reeked of gases, powder, and decaying matter. Shells were constantly bursting overhead, and in places the trenches had crumbled and were nearly blocked up. They stumbled on, sometimes falling, sometimes dodging moving masses, and occasionally crawling over the dead bodies of men. At last they reached a deserted-looking trench, and one of the soldiers pushed him into the corner of it and growled something, and then disappeared round the angle. Old Sam was ex-exhausted. He leaned panting against the mud wall, expecting every minute to be blown to pieces by one of those infernal things that seemed to be getting more and more insistent. The din went on for nearly twenty minutes, and he was alone in the trench. He fancied he heard a whistle amidst the din. Suddenly one of the soldiers who had accompanied him came stealthily round the corner, and there was a look in his eye old Sam did not like. When he was within five yards the soldier raised his rifle and pointed it at Sam's body. Some instinct impelled the old man at that instant to throw himself forward on his face. As he did so he was aware of a terrible explosion, and he had just time to observe the soldier falling in a heap near him, and then he lost consciousness.

His consciousness appeared to return to him with a snap. He was lying on a plank in a building, and he heard some one say:

"I believe the old boy's English."

He looked round. There were a lot of men lying there, and others in khaki and white overalls were busy among them. He sat up, rubbed his head, and said:

"Hi, Mister, where be I now?"

Some one laughed, and a young man came up and said:

"Well, old man, you were very nearly in hell. Who the devil are you?"

Some one came up, and two of them were discussing him. One of them said:

"He's quite all right. He was only knocked out. Better take him in to the colonel. He may be a spy."

The other came up, touched his shoulder. and remarked:

"Can you walk, Uncle?"

He replied:

"Aye, I can walk all roight."

"That's an old sport!"

The young man took his arm and helped him out of the room into a courtyard. They entered another room, where an elderly, kind-faced officer was seated at a desk. The officer looked up and exclaimed:

"Good God! Bradshaw, do you know who you've got there?"

The younger one said:

"No. Who, sir?"

"It's Paul Jouperts!" exclaimed the colonel.

"Paul Jouperts! Great Scott!"

The older officer addressed himself to Sam. He said:

"Well, we've got you once more, Paul. We shall have to be a little more careful this time."

The young officer said:

"Shall I detail a squad, sir?"

"We can't shoot him without a court-martial," replied the kind-faced senior.

Then Sam interpolated:

"Look 'ee 'ere, sir, I'm fair' sick of all this. My name bean 't Paul. My name 's Sam. I was a-thinnin' a loine o' turnips—"

Both officers burst out laughing, and the younger one said:

"Good! damn good! Isn't it amazing, sir, the way they not only learn the language, but even take the trouble to learn a dialect!"

The older man busied himself with some papers.

"Well, Sam," he remarked, "you shall be given a chance to prove your identity. Our methods are less drastic than those of your *Boche* masters. What

part of England are you supposed to come from? Let
's see how much you can bluff us with your topo-
graphical knowledge."

"I was a-thinnin' a loine o' turnips this mornin' at
'alf-past seven on Mr. Hodge's farm at Halvesham
when one o' these 'ere airyplanes come down among
the swedes. I tells 'e to get clear o' that, when the
feller what gets out o' the car 'e drahs a revowlver
and 'e says, 'You must 'company I—'"

"Yes, yes," interrupted the senior officer; "that 's
all very good. Now tell me—where is Halvesham?
What is the name of the local vicar? I 'm sure you
'd know that."

Old Sam rubbed his chin.

"I sits under the Reverend David Pryce, Mister,
and a good, God-fearin' man he be. I took him a
cookin' o' runner beans on'y yesterday. I works for
Mr. Hodge, what owns Greenway Manor and 'as a
stud-farm at Newmarket, they say."

"Charles Hodge?" asked the young officer.

"Aye, Charlie Hodge. You write and ask un if
he knows old Sam Gates."

The two officers looked at each other, and the older
one looked at Sam more closely.

"It 's very extraordinary," he remarked.

"Everybody knows Charlie Hodge," added the
younger officer.

It was at that moment that a wave of genius swept
over old Sam. He put his hand to his head and
suddenly jerked out:

"What 's more, I can tell 'ee where this yere Paul
is. He 's actin' a gardener in a convent at—" He
puckered up his brows, fumbled with his hat, and then
got out, "Mighteno."

The older officer gasped

"Mailleton-en-haut! Good God! what makes you say that, old man?"

Sam tried to give an account of his experience and the things he had heard said by the German officers; but he was getting tired, and he broke off in the middle to say:

"Ye have n't a bite o' somethin' to eat, I suppose, Mister; or a glass o' beer? I usually 'as my dinner at twelve o'clock."

Both the officers laughed, and the older said:

"Get him some food, Bradshaw, and a bottle of beer from the mess. We'll keep this old man here. He interests me."

While the younger man was doing this, the chief pressed a button and summoned another junior officer.

"Gateshead," he remarked, "ring up the G. H. Q. and instruct them to arrest the gardener in that convent at the top of the hill and then to report."

The officer saluted and went out, and in a few minutes a tray of hot food and a large bottle of beer were brought to the old man, and he was left alone in the corner of the room to negotiate this welcome compensation. And in the execution he did himself and his county credit. In the meanwhile the officers were very busy. People were coming and going and examining maps, and telephone bells were ringing furiously. They did not disturb old Sam's gastric operations. He cleaned up the mess tins and finished the last drop of beer. The senior officer found time to offer him a cigaret, but he replied:

"Thank 'ee kindly, sir, but I'd rather smoke my pipe."

The colonel smiled and said:

"Oh, all right; smoke away."

He lighted up, and the fumes of the shag permea[
the room. Some one opened another window, [
the young officer who had addressed him at f[
suddenly looked at him and exclaimed:

"Innocent, by God! You couldn't get shag [
that anywhere but in Norfolk."

It must have been an hour later when another offi
entered and saluted.

"Message from the G. H. Q., sir," he said.

"Well?"

"They have arrested the gardener at the conv[
of St. Eloise, and they have every reason to beli[
that he is the notorious Paul Jouperts."

The colonel stood up, and his eyes beamed. [
came over to old Sam and shook his hand.

"Mr. Gates," he said, "you are an old brick. Y[
will probably hear more of this. You have proba[
been the means of delivering something very us[
into our hands. Your own honor is vindicated. [
loving Government will probably award you [
shillings or a Victoria Cross or something of that s[
In the meantime, what can I do for you?"

Old Sam scratched his chin.

"I want to get back 'ome," he said.

"Well, even that might be arranged."

"I want to get back 'ome in toime for tea."

"What time do you have tea?"

"Foive o'clock or thereabouts."

"I see."

A kindly smile came into the eyes of the colo[
He turned to another officer standing by the t[
and said:

"Raikes, is any one going across this afternoon with dispatches?"

"Yes, sir," replied the other officer. "Commander Jennings is leaving at three o'clock."

"You might ask him if he could see me."

Within ten minutes a young man in a flight-commander's uniform entered.

"Ah, Jennings," said the colonel, "here is a little affair which concerns the honor of the British army. My friend here, Sam Gates, has come over from Halvesham, in Norfolk, in order to give us valuable information. I have promised him that he shall get home to tea at five o'clock. Can you take a passenger?"

The young man threw back his head and laughed.

"Lord!" he exclaimed, "what an old sport! Yes, I expect I can manage it. Where is the God-forsaken place?"

A large ordnance-map of Norfolk (which had been captured from a German officer) was produced, and the young man studied it closely.

At three o'clock precisely old Sam, finding himself something of a hero and quite glad to escape from the embarrassment which this position entailed upon him, once more sped skyward in a "dratted airyplane."

At twenty minutes to five he landed once more among Mr. Hodge's swedes. The breezy young airman shook hands with him and departed inland. Old Sam sat down and surveyed the familiar field of turnips.

"A noice thing, I must say!" he muttered to himself as he looked along the lines of unthinned turnips. He still had twenty minutes, and so he went slowly along and completed a line which he had begun in the morning. He then deliberately packed up his dinner-things and his tools and started out for home.

As he came round the corner of Stillway's meadow and the cottage came in view, his niece stepped out of the copse with a basket on her arm.

"Well, Uncle," she said, "is there any noos?"

It was then that old Sam really lost his temper.

"Noos!" he said. "Noos! Drat the girl! What noos should there be? Sixty-nine year' I live in these 'ere parts, hoein' and weedin' and thinnin', and mindin' Charlie Hodge's sheep. Am I one o' these 'ere story-book folk havin' noos 'appen to me all the time? Ain't it enough, ye silly, dab-faced zany, to earn enough to buy a bite o' some' to eat and a glass o' beer and a place to rest a's head o'night without always wantin' noos, noos, noos! I tell 'ee it 's this that leads 'ee to 'alf the troubles in the world. Devil take the noos!"

And turning his back on her, he went fuming up the hill.

MATEO FALCONE

By Prosper Merimee

On leaving Porto-Vecchio from the northwest and
directing his steps towards the interior of the island,
the traveller will notice that the land rises rapidly,
and after three hours' walking over tortuous paths
obstructed by great masses of rock and sometimes
cut by ravines, he will find himself on the border of
a great mâquis. The mâquis is the domain of the
Corsican shepherds and of those who are at variance
with justice. It must be known that, in order to save
himself the trouble of manuring his field, the Corsican
husbandman sets fire to a piece of woodland. If
the flame spread farther than is necessary, so much
the worse! In any case he is certain of a good crop
from the land fertilized by the ashes of the trees
which grow upon it. He gathers only the heads of his
grain, leaving the straw, which it would be unnecessary
labor to cut. In the following spring the roots that
have remained in the earth without being destroyed
send up their tufts of sprouts, which in a few years
reach a height of seven or eight feet. It is this kind
of tangled thicket that is called a mâquis. They are
made up of different kinds of trees and shrubs, so
crowded and mingled together at the caprice of nature
that only with an ax in hand can a man open a
passage through them, and mâquis are frequently seen

so thick and bushy that the wild sheep themselves cannot penetrate them.

If you have killed a man, go into the mâquis of Porto-Vecchio. With a good gun and plenty of powder and balls, you can live there in safety. Do not forget a brown cloak furnished with a hood, which will serve you for both cover and mattress. The shepherds will give you chestnuts, milk and cheese, and you will have nothing to fear from justice nor the relatives of the dead except when it is necessary for you to descend to the city to replenish your ammunition.

When I was in Corsica in 18—, Mateo Falcone had his house half a league from this mâquis. He was rich enough for that country, living in noble style— that is to say, doing nothing—on the income from his flocks, which the shepherds, who are a kind of nomads, lead to pasture here and there on the mountains. When I saw him, two years after the event that I am about to relate, he appeared to me to be about fifty years old or more. Picture to yourself a man, small but robust, with curly hair, black as jet, an aquiline nose, thin lips, large, restless eyes, and a complexion the color of tanned leather. His skill as a marksman was considered extraordinary even in his country, where good shots are so common. For example, Mateo would never fire at a sheep with buckshot; but at a hundred and twenty paces, he would drop it with a ball in the head or shoulder, as he chose. He used his arms as easily at night as during the day. I was told this feat of his skill, which will, perhaps, seem impossible to those who have not travelled in Corsica. A lighted candle was placed at eighty paces, behind a paper transparency about the size of a plate. He would take aim, then the candle would be extinguished,

and, at the end of a moment, in the most complete
darkness, he would fire and hit the paper three times
out of four.

With such a transcendent accomplishment, Mateo
Falcone had acquired a great reputation. He was said
to be as good a friend as he was a dangerous enemy;
accommodating and charitable, he lived at peace with
all the world in the district of Porto-Vecchio. But it
is said of him that in Corte, where he had married
his wife, he had disembarrassed himself very vigorously
of a rival who was considered as redoubtable in war
as in love; at least, a certain gun-shot which surprized
this rival as he was shaving before a little mirror hung
in his window was attributed to Mateo. The affair
was smoothed over and Mateo was married. His wife
Giuseppa had given him at first three daughters (which
infuriated him), and finally a son, whom he named
Fortunato, and who became the hope of his family,
the inheritor of the name. The daughters were well
married: their father could count at need on the
poignards and carbines of his sons-in-law. The son
was only ten years old, but he already gave promise
of fine attributes.

On a certain day in autumn, Mateo set out at an
early hour with his wife to visit one of his flocks in
a clearing of the mâquis. The little Fortunato wanted
to go with them, but the clearing was too far away;
moreover, it was necessary some one should stay to
watch the house; therefore the father refused: it will
be seen whether or not he had reason to repent.

He had been gone some hours, and the little Fortunato was tranquilly stretched out in the sun, looking
at the blue mountains, and thinking that the next
Sunday he was going to dine in the city with his uncle,

the Caporal,[1] when he was suddenly interrupted in
his meditations by the firing of a musket. He got
up and turned to that side of the plain whence the noise
came. Other shots followed, fired at irregular intervals,
and each time nearer; at last, in the path which led
from the plain to Mateo's house, appeared a man
wearing the pointed hat of the mountaineers, bearded,
covered with rags, and dragging himself along with
difficulty by the support of his gun. He had just
received a wound in his thigh.

This man was an outlaw, who, having gone to the
town by night to buy powder, had fallen on the way
into an ambuscade of Corsican light-infantry. After
a vigorous defense he was fortunate in making his
retreat, closely followed and firing from rock to rock.
But he was only a little in advance of the soldiers, and
his wound prevented him from gaining the mâquis
before being overtaken.

He approached Fortunato and said: "You are the
son of Mateo Falcone?"—"Yes."

"I am Gianetto Saupiero. I am followed by the
yellow-collars.[2] Hide me, for I can go no farther."

"And what will my father say if I hide you without
his permission?"

"He will say that you have done well."

"How do you know?"

"Hide me quickly; they are coming."

"Wait till my father gets back."

"How can I wait? Malediction! They will be
here in five minutes. Come, hide me, or I will kill
you."

Fortunato answered him with the utmost coolness:

---

[1] Civic Official.
[2] Slang for Gendarmes.

"Your gun is empty, and there are no more cartridges in your belt."

"I have my stiletto."

"But can you run as fast as I can?"

He gave a leap and put himself out of reach.

"You are not the son of Mateo Falcone! Will you then let me be captured before your house?"

The child appeared moved.

"What will you give me if I hide you?" said he, coming nearer.

The outlaw felt in a leather pocket that hung from his belt, and took out a five-franc piece, which he had doubtless saved to buy ammunition with. Fortunato smiled at the sight of the silver piece; he snatched it, and said to Gianetto:

"Fear nothing."

Immediately he made a great hole in a pile of hay that was near the house. Gianetto crouched down in it and the child covered him in such a way that he could breathe without it being possible to suspect that the hay concealed a man. He bethought himself further, and, with the subtlety of a tolerably ingenious savage, placed a cat and her kittens on the pile, that it might not appear to have been recently disturbed. Then, noticing the traces of blood on the path near the house, he covered them carefully with dust, and, that done, he again stretched himself out in the sun with the greatest tranquillity.

A few moments afterwards, six men in brown uniforms with yellow collars, and commanded by an Adjutant, were before Mateo's door. This Adjutant was a distant relative of Falcone's. (In Corsica the degrees of relationship are followed much further than elsewhere.) His name was Tiodoro Gamba; he was an active man, much dreaded by the outlaws, several of whom he had already entrapped.

"Good day, little cousin," said he, approaching Fortunato; "how tall you have grown. Have you seen a man go past here just now?"

"Oh! I am not yet so tall as you, my cousin," replied the child with a simple air.

"You soon will be. But haven't you seen a man go by here, tell me?"

"If I have seen a man go by?"

"Yes, a man with a pointed hat of black velvet, and a vest embroidered with red and yellow."

"A man with a pointed hat, and a vest embroidered with red and yellow?"

"Yes, answer quickly, and don't repeat my questions?"

"This morning the curé passed before our door on his horse, Piero. He asked me how papa was, and I answered him——"

"Ah, you little scoundrel, you are playing sly! Tell me quickly which way Gianetto went? We are looking for him, and I am sure he took this path."

"Who knows?"

"Who knows? It is I know that you have seen him."

"Can any one see who passes when they are asleep?"

"You were not asleep, rascal; the shooting woke you up."

"Then you believe, cousin, that your guns make so much noise? My father's carbine has the advantage of them."

"The devil take you, you cursed little scapegrace! I am certain that you have seen Gianetto. Perhaps, even, you have hidden him. Come, comrades, go into

the house and see if our man is there. He could only
go on one foot, and the knave has too much good
sense to try to reach the mâquis limping like that.
Moreover, the bloody tracks stop here."

"And what will papa say?" asked Fortunato with
a sneer; "what will he say if he knows that his house
has been entered while he was away?"

"You rascal!" said the Adjutant, taking him by the
ear, "do you know that it only remains for me to make
you change your tone? Perhaps you will speak dif-
ferently after I have given you twenty blows with
the flat of my sword."

Fortunato continued to sneer.

"My father is Mateo Falcone," said he with
emphasis.

"You little scamp, you know very well that I can
carry you off to Corte or to Bastia. I will make you
lie in a dungeon, on straw, with your feet in shackles,
and I will have you guillotined if you don't tell me
where Gianetto is."

The child burst out laughing at this ridiculous
menace. He repeated:

"My father is Mateo Falcone."

"Adjutant," said one of the soldiers in a low voice,
"let us have no quarrels with Mateo."

Gamba appeared evidently embarrassed. He spoke
in an undertone with the soldiers who had already
visited the house. This was not a very long operation,
for the cabin of a Corsican consists only of a single
square room, furnished with a table, some benches,
chests, housekeeping utensils and those of the chase.
In the meantime, little Fortunato petted his cat and
seemed to take a wicked enjoyment in the confusion
of the soldiers and of his cousin.

One of the men approached the pile of hay. He saw the cat, and gave the pile a careless thrust with his bayonet, shrugging his shoulders as if he felt that his precaution was ridiculous. Nothing moved; the boy's face betrayed not the slightest emotion.

The Adjutant and his troop were cursing their luck. Already they were looking in the direction of the plain, as if disposed to return by the way they had come, when their chief convinced that menaces would produce no impression on Falcone's son, determined to make a last effort, and try the effect of caresses and presents.

"My little cousin," said he, "you are a very wide-awake little fellow. You will get along. But you are playing a naughty game with me; and if I wasn't afraid of making trouble for my cousin, Mateo, the devil take me! but I would carry you off with me."

"Bah!"

"But when my cousin comes back I shall tell him about this, and he will whip you till the blood comes for having told such lies."

"You don't say so!"

"You will see. But hold on!—be a good boy and I will give you something."

"Cousin, let me give you some advice: if you wait much longer Gianetto will be in the mâquis and it will take a smarter man than you to follow him."

The Adjutant took from his pocket a silver watch worth about ten crowns, and noticing that Fortunato's eyes sparkled at the sight of it, said, holding the watch by the end of its steel chain:

"Rascal! you would like to have such a watch as that hung around your neck, wouldn't you, and to walk in the streets of Porto-Vecchio proud as a peacock? People would ask you what time it was, and you would say: 'Look at my watch.'"

"When I am grown up, my uncle, the Caporal, will give me a watch."

"Yes; but your uncle's little boy has one already; not so fine as this either. But then, he is younger than you."

The child sighed.

"Well! Would you like this watch, little cousin?"

Fortunato, casting sidelong glances at the watch, resembled a cat that has been given a whole chicken. It feels that it is being made sport of, and does not dare to use its claws; from time to time it turns its eyes away so as not to be tempted, licking its jaws all the while, and has the appearance of saying to its master, "How cruel your joke is!"

However, the Adjutant seemed in earnest in offering his watch. Fortunato did not reach out his hand for it, but said with a bitter smile:

"Why do you make fun of me?"

"Good God! I am not making fun of you. Only tell me where Gianetto is and the watch is yours."

Fortunato smiled incredulously, and fixing his black eyes on those of the Adjutant tried to read there the faith he ought to have had in his words.

"May I lose my epaulets," cried the Adjutant, "if I do not give you the watch on this condition. These comrades are witnesses; I can not deny it."

While speaking he gradually held the watch nearer till it almost touched the child's pale face, which plainly showed the struggle that was going on in his soul between covetousness and respect for hospitality. His breast swelled with emotion; he seemed about to suffocate. Meanwhile the watch was slowly swaying

and turning, sometimes brushing against his cheek.
Finally, his right hand was gradually stretched toward
it; the ends of his fingers touched it; then its whole
weight was in his hand, the Adjutant still keeping
hold of the chain. The face was light blue; the cases
newly burnished. In the sunlight it seemed to be all
on fire. The temptation was too great. Fortunato
raised his left hand and pointed over his shoulder
with his thumb at the hay against which he was
reclining. The Adjutant understood him at once. He
dropped the end of the chain and Fortunato felt himself the sole possessor of the watch. He sprang up
with the agility of a deer and stood ten feet from the
pile, which the soldiers began at once to overturn.

There was a movement in the hay, and a bloody man
with a poignard in his hand appeared. He tried to
rise to his feet, but his stiffened leg would not permit
it and he fell. The Adjutant at once grappled with
him and took away his stiletto. He was immediately
secured, notwithstanding his resistance.

Gianetto, lying on the earth and bound like a fagot,
turned his head towards Fortunato, who had approached.

"Son of—!" said he, with more contempt than
anger.

The child threw him the silver piece which he had
received, feeling that he no longer deserved it; but
the outlaw paid no attention to the movement, and
with great coolness said to the Adjutant:

"My dear Gamba, I cannot walk; you will be
obliged to carry me to the city."

"Just now you could run faster than a buck," answered the cruel captor; "but be at rest. I am so
pleased to have you that I would carry you a league
on my back without fatigue. Besides, comrade, we

are going to make a litter for you with your cloak and some branches, and at the Crespoli farm we shall find horses."

"Good," said the prisoner. "You will also put a little straw on your litter that I may be more comfortable."

While some of the soldiers were occupied in making a kind of stretcher out of some chestnut boughs and the rest were dressing Gianetto's wound, Mateo Falcone and his wife suddenly appeared at a turn in the path that led to the mâquis. The woman was staggering under the weight of an enormous sack of chestnuts, while her husband was sauntering along, carrying one gun in his hands, while another was slung across his shoulders, for it is unworthy of a man to carry other burdens than his arms.

At the sight of the soldiers Mateo's first thought was that they had come to arrest him. But why this thought? Had he then some quarrels with justice? No. He enjoyed a good reputation. He was said to have a particularly good name, but he was a Corsican and a highlander, and there are few Corsican highlanders who, in scrutinizing their memory, can not find some peccadillo, such as a gun-shot, dagger-thrust, or similar trifles. Mateo more than others had a clear conscience; for more than ten years he had not pointed his carbine at a man, but he was always prudent, and put himself into a position to make a good defense if necessary. "Wife," said he to Giuseppa, "put down the sack and hold yourself ready."

She obeyed at once. He gave her the gun that was slung across his shoulders, which would have bothered him, and, cocking the one he held in his hands, advanced slowly towards the house, walking among the trees that bordered the road, ready at the least hostile demonstration, to hide behind the largest, whence he could fire from under cover. His wife followed closely behind, holding his reserve weapon and his cartridge-box. The duty of a good housekeeper, in case of a fight, is to load her husband's carbines.

On the other side the Adjutant was greatly troubled to see Mateo advance in this manner, with cautious steps, his carbine raised, and his finger on the trigger. "If by chance," thought he, "Mateo should be related to Gianetto, or if he should be his friend and wish to defend him, the contents of his two guns would arrive amongst us as certainly as a letter in the post; and if he should see me, notwithstanding the relationship!"

In this perplexity he took a bold step. It was to advance alone towards Mateo and tell him of the affair while accosting him as an old acquaintance, but the short space that separated him from Mateo seemed terribly long.

"Hello! old comrade," cried he. "How do you do, my good fellow? It is I, Gamba, your cousin."

Without answering a word, Mateo stopped, and in proportion as the other spoke, slowly raised the muzzle of his gun so that it was pointing upward when the Adjutant joined him.

"Good-day, brother," said the Adjutant, holding out his hand. "It is a long time since I have seen you."

"Good-day, brother."

"I stopped while passing, to say good-day to you and to cousin Pepa here. We have had a long journey to-day, but have no reason to complain, for we have captured a famous prize. We have just seized Gianetto Saupiero."

"God be praised!" cried Giuseppa. "He stole a milch goat from us last week."

These words reassured Gamba.

"Poor devil!" said Mateo, "he was hungry."

"The villain fought like a lion," continued the Adjutant, a little mortified. "He killed one of my soldiers, and not content with that, broke Caporal Chardon's arm; but that matters little, he is only a Frenchman. Then, too, he was so well hidden that the devil couldn't have found him. Without my little cousin, Fortunato, I should never have discovered him."

"Fortunato!" cried Mateo.

"Fortunato!" repeated Giuseppa.

"Yes, Gianetto was hidden under the hay-pile yonder, but my little cousin showed me the trick. I shall tell his uncle, the Caporal, that he may send him a fine present for his trouble. Both his name and yours will be in the report that I shall send to the Attorney-general."

"Malediction!" said Mateo in a low voice.

They had rejoined the detachment. Gianetto was already lying on the litter ready to set out. When he saw Mateo and Gamba in company he smiled a strange smile, then, turning his head towards the door of the house, he spat on the sill, saying:

"House of a traitor."

Only a man determined to die would dare pronounce the word traitor to Falcone. A good blow with the stiletto, which there would be no need of repeating, would have immediately paid the insult. However, Mateo made no other movement than to place his hand on his forehead like a man who is dazed.

Fortunato had gone into the house when his father arrived, but now he reappeared with a bowl of milk which he handed with downcast eyes to Gianetto.

"Get away from me!" cried the outlaw, in a loud voice. Then, turning to one of the soldiers, he said: "Comrade, give me a drink."

The soldier placed his gourd in his hands, and the prisoner drank the water handed to him by a man with whom he had just exchanged bullets. He then asked them to tie his hands across his breast instead of behind his back.

"I like," said he, "to lie at my ease."

They hastened to satisfy him; then the Adjutant gave the signal to start, said adieu to Mateo, who did not respond, and descended with rapid steps towards the plain.

Nearly ten minutes elapsed before Mateo spoke. The child looked with restless eyes, now at his mother, now at his father, who was leaning on his gun and gazing at him with an expression of concentrated rage.

"You begin well," said Mateo at last with a calm voice, but frightful to one who knew the man.

"Oh, father!" cried the boy, bursting into tears, and making a forward movement as if to throw himself on his knees. But Mateo cried, "Away from me!"

The little fellow stopped and sobbed, immovable, a few feet from his father.

Giuseppa drew near. She had just discovered the watch-chain, the end of which was hanging out of Fortunato's jacket.

"Who gave you that watch?" demanded she in a severe tone.

"My cousin, the Adjutant."

Falcone seized the watch and smashed it in a thousand pieces against a rock.

"Wife," said he, "is this my child?"

Giuseppa's cheeks turned a brick-red.

"What are you saying, Mateo? Do you know to whom you speak?"

"Very well, this child is the first of his race to commit treason."

Fortunato's sobs and gasps redoubled as Falcone kept his lynx-eyes upon him. Then he struck the earth with his gunstock, shouldered the weapon, and turned in the direction of the mâquis, calling to Fortunato to follow. The boy obeyed. Giuseppa hastened after Mateo and seized his arm.

"He is your son," said she with a trembling voice, fastening her black eyes on those of her husband to read what was going on in his heart.

"Leave me alone," said Mateo, "I am his father."

Gieuseppa embraced her son, and bursting into tears entered the house. She threw herself on her knees before an image of the Virgin and prayed ardently. In the meanwhile Falcone walked some two hundred paces along the path and only stopped when he reached a little ravine which he descended. He tried the earth with the butt-end of his carbine, and found it soft and easy to dig. The place seemed to be convenient for his design.

"Fortunato, go close to that big rock there."

The child did as he was commanded, then he kneeled.

"Say your prayers."

"Oh, father, father, do not kill me!"

"Say your prayers!" repeated Mateo in a terrible voice.

The boy, stammering and sobbing, recited the Pater and the Credo. At the end of each prayer the father loudly answered, "Amen!"

"Are those all the prayers you know?"

"Oh! father, I know the Ave Maria and the litany that my aunt taught me."

"It is very long, but no matter."

The child finished the litany in a scarcely audible tone.

"Are you finished?"

"Oh! my father, have mercy! Pardon me! I will never do so again. I will beg my cousin, the Caporal, to pardon Gianetto."

He was still speaking. Mateo raised his gun, and, taking aim, said:

"May God pardon you!"

The boy made a desperate effort to rise and grasp his father's knees, but there was not time. Mateo fired and Fortunato fell dead.

Without casting a glance on the body, Mateo returned to the house for a spade with which to bury his son. He had gone but a few steps when he met Giuseppa, who, alarmed by the shot, was hastening hither.

"What have you done?" cried she.

"Justice."

"Where is he?"

"In the ravine. I am going to bury him. He died a Christian. I shall have a mass said for him Have my son-in-law, Tiodoro Bianchi, sent for to come and live with us."

THE QUEER SCARE

By James Hopper

The Cowdrays had been in the settlement only a few months, and of evenings, sometimes, they would feel lonely. This was because they were from the "East," and had lived most of their lives in great stone cities, with millions of people ever about them, while now their rustic cottage—bungalow it was called in this land—stood frail and solitary in a pine forest by the shore of an immense ocean.

True, only five miles away was a very live little town. But these five miles were over a hill as high almost as a mountain, along a winding road skirting cañons, between high, dark trees; and then that town was two hundred and fifty miles from the nearest city; and that city days and days, mountains and plains away from the real world they had known. So sitting in the evening, with small Clare playing on the carpet between them, they could see the cottage all too clearly, frail and alone in the pines, by the great sea, so far from the nearest town, in turn so far from the nearest city, in turn so far from the real world. A weight of loneliness fell upon them, and they would be apt to say: "Let's go over to the Burtons' for a minute, what do you say?"

They would then look at each other in dim hesitation, while little Clare, after one quick upward glance,

179

resumed her playing in a slightly different manner now, with light temporary gestures, as if waiting.

In that little white wisp of a child, in a way, there was a sort of punishment for the Cowdrays—a punishment for ignoble Prudence. Once they had not thought of it as Prudence. They had thought of it as intelligence and foresight, and proud desire to live their lives. Now they know it had been but Prudence. Their child had come late in their marriage, and now they were being punished by a tenderness which was like an ache, which at times was almost intolerable. Oh, they could have had it long, that sweet delicate Happiness, and they had refused it. Oh, oh, it might be taken away from them—and then they could never have it any more. Their tenderness was shredded with pain, was shredded with fear.

"Well, what do you say? Shall we go?"

But they still hesitated, altho as, in the great stillness, the child played so like a candle flame, they had come to one of those almost unbearable moments. Over there, at the Burtons', it would be different. You did not hear yourself so much over there—you did not feel yourself so much.

Young Burton—his cottage was not a place in solitude at the confines of the earth. He worked in the small town five miles away, and his cottage, to him, was a tight and cozy little suburban home for himself and his young wife. And a suburban home it was like. Built as if on a thirty-foot lot instead of a spot in the wilderness, with thousands of free miles on all sides. And resolutely urban, plastered, with tight windows, compact, the kitchen a kitchenette.

Passing from here to there was like passing from one

sphere to another. From one a little too rarefied, of sensibilities too taut, to one a bit cheap and loud, but warm—and safe. Realities were close about you there; you were safe.

Even the radio. Burton's beloved radio—

The radio, Cowdray thought, that incredible thing! A sound was sent out at one end, far, far, far. It was killed, it was transformed, it was etherealized, it became a ghost. Across, over the land, far, far, far, through the clear, high air, athwart the stars, it winged, a ghost. It arrived—presto, it was materialized—it became sound again.

The trouble was this sound would be "Oh, red-hot mama, red-hot mama—yap, yap, yap; yap, yap, yap." Or sickly ukulelian strains. Or the politician's sonorities: "I take pleasure in prresenting to-night, one of this na-a-tion's most ster-r-r-r-ling Dem-ocrats. Yap, yap, yap; wow, wow, wow."

Young Burton, he was a radio fan. His radio was always going. When you called, all the time it kept going. "Red-Hot Mama." "I take the greatest pleasure in presenting—"

Never mind. A good place to go to when this silence came. This silence in this room, and small Clare playing with her "precious little things." Playing so quietly in the silence. How slender and white she was! A little white flame.

"Well, shall we go?"

The mother sprang to her feet. "Yes, let's go."

"I'm going to take my toys," said Clare.

She was gathering them up. As tho the river were rising, as tho inundation threatened! "All my little precious things," she said. These were little chairs, little tables, little beds, a little lamp, a little motor

car, a little gramophone—tiny dwarfish toys from
Japan. As she played with them, one had an eerie
feeling she had slipped off into another world entirely,
a little, delicate, gnomish world, out of this one of
gross things. "I'll take Madge too," she said. "And
that bad cat, Miserocrocis."

She held them with her folded arms against her
little breast, and went out first as they closed the
door behind. The way was along a dim road beneath
the pines, with here and there a bluish splash from
the setting crescent moon. Soon the Burton house
showed, all compact, all lit up. "Yes," Cowdray
murmured, "the radio is going." And before they
entered, they could see, through the living-room
window, Burton and his young wife sitting there,
playing cards, with the radio horn turned upon them,
flooding them.

There were cries, scrapings of chairs. What simple,
sincere, warm folk, the Burtons! How true their welcome, the liking you felt beneath! "We've just
dropped in for a minute," cried the Cowdrays, but in
every posture and every gesture the Burtons said,
"You can stay forever."

"Forever!" sang the radio. "Fo-o-o-o-r Ever!"

For, of course, the radio was still going. Naturally,
since the Burtons were radio mad. Small Clare was
already installed, on the carpet, absorbed in her eerie
minute toys—it was as if she had not moved: as if
she were still at the other house. The others sat
about her in their chairs. What a little white flame
she was! But it was better here, in this house. Even
the vulgarity helped, and Burton's over-rotund cordiality. Even the yelping radio. Over there, in that
other house, all alone, they got, well—it was a bit

maudlin—that pain of tenderness for the child; the uneasiness: almost morbid it was.

Burton was having trouble with the radio. He kept rising and going to it. He kept turning metal knobs. "It isn't going very well to-night," he apologized. The radio was his child. "Interference," he grandly and vaguely explained. "Static," he announced.

Suddenly a thin, sweet strain came floating into the room. "Violin," thought Cowdray. "Martini's Pastorale. Martini, Padre Martini. The priest musician. Seventeenth century."

But the violinist (where was he—miles and miles away?) was not of the first order. He sentimentalized. He forced heavy sobs into the frail, fine, wistful music.

"Imagine," thought Cowdray. "The padre's soul in the ether. Spread out thin and sentient throughout the ether. And that coming through it—his own song, played like that—tearing through it, through his soul. He must suffer!"

"Rr-rr-rrrrrrrrrrrrrrrrrr!" Went the radio. "Rr-rr-rrrrrrrrrr!" A sort of terrific dry roar, cutting like a buzz-saw through the slender music. And then again, "rrrrrrrrrrrrrrr!" As if some great sidereal beast were snarling in the great void.

Burton shook his head in concern. Again, several times, came the heavy, brutal interruptions, which somehow left them all tense, with tight nerves.

"Tremendously dramatic," Cowdray thought.

"It's the fleet," said Burton. "The war fleet on maneuvers. They're going out of San Francisco to-night. They use those big currents. Tear the deuce out of ours."

And sitting there, they all saw, far off yet close at hand, the big steel hulls nosing out of the Golden Gate into the dark, limitless sea. Signaling imperiously to each other: "Where are you?" "Here, here." "Where? *Where?*" "Here—here." "And you—where? Speak I say—*where?*" "Here—can't you hear? Here, here!"

"Rr-rr-rr-rrrrrrrrrrrrrrrr!" Their voices were of steel. They tore the gentle padre's music to bleeding tatters.

"It's the fleet," Burton repeated. "The war fleet, putting out to sea. They use those big currents. Gee—they certainly rip things up!"

But just then the radio went dead. The gentle music ceased and the savage interruptions: both at once, in a silence that seemed stunningly complete.

"What the deuce!" said Burton, with the effect of one speaking suddenly in the dark.

He rose, turned knobs, adjusted wires—but no sound came from the box, not a rustle, not a sigh.

He gave it up. "Can you beat it? She's gone dead on me. Absolutely dead."

But he could not believe it. He was up again, turning knobs, trying adjustments. Once more he sat down, baffled. "No—she's dead," he said. 'By golly, she is. Absolutely dead!"

But now the little girl, who all the time had played on the carpet, absorbed in her eerie little toys, froze to immobility and seemed to give ear. She rose, and with three dancing steps was at the radio.

"Yes?" she hallooed softly. "Yes?"

Then, "Yes, I am here. Yes, I hear."

"Clare," her mother cried. "Stop that, stop that—you know you are hearing nothing! Stop it!"

"Yes," chimed Cowdray, a strange prickly feeling along his spine. "Come here, Clare!"

But the child, still poised, still gave ear. "Oh, yes!" she cried. "Yes, yes, yes. That is very nice. Oh, I'm glad! Yes, I will. Some time, I will. Yes."

She listened a moment longer, gave three serious little nods, then a bit languidly came back to her toys, slipped to the carpet, and was playing again.

There was a long silence. Each in the room formulated in his mind a sentence which somehow he or she did not pronounce.

"Maybe there was a murmur in the radio," Burton thought. "Children's ears are so sharp."

"What a little actress!" thought Mrs. Burton. "Almost scared me to death!"

But Helen Cowdray's unspoken thought was a turbulent question, which beat in rhythm with her heart. "What was it, what was it, dear? What was it, what was it, what was it?"

When the Cowdrays started homeward the moon had set, the night was dark, but the stars shone bright through the trees. Clare walked along for a little while; then she stopped in a manner her father well knew. "Want to be carried, sweet?" And without waiting for the answer he stooped and raised her in his arms.

Up there, drooping a little, her flower face in his neck, she grew confidential. "Would you like to know who talked to me on the radio, Daddy?" she whispered.

"Yes. Who was it?"

"He was a little boy—far, far, far off. He said, 'I see you, Clare.' He said, 'Clare, do you hear me?' I said, 'Yes, yes, yes.' He said, 'Little Clare, I love you.' I said, 'That's very nice.' He said, 'Some time may I come for you?' And I said, 'Yes, yes, yes.' Wasn't that nice, Daddy?"

"Who was the little boy?" he said, meaning it playfully, but finding his throat absurdly tight.

"A little boy away off. In a star. *That* star, Daddy."

In the darkness he could see her finger raised, with its baby crook, toward a star—a star, a bit red, in the center of a clearing of the trees.

When they reached the cottage door the child had gone to sleep, lax like a culled flower, across his shoulder, and the mother eagerly whispered. "What star was that, John?"

He gave a short laugh. "Not a bad choice, for a chance shot. It was Mars."

The mother began to tremble; he could feel her trembling against him. "John—you don't think there can be anything like that—do you, John? It's just her play, isn't it? There *can't* be anything like that, can there?"

"Why-y, of course not! Why, you poor thing, all a-tremble! Why, of course not! What nonsense!"

But something within him mutely was booming: "What do we know? What do we know? We know nothing, we know nothing. Anything is possible, anything!"

"I'm frightened, John. It's foolish—but I'm frightened. Tell me again. There couldn't be anything like that, could there? A—something—somewhere—that would want her— Oh, John, I'm so frightened!"

He made his voice deep with sonorous reassurance. "Of course not, of course not."

The door was now open; he switched on the lights

as they went in. That darkness—how silly people got in the darkness. Here it was all golden glow.

He carried the child across the living-room to her small chamber, dropped her to the bed. Together they put her to bed, kissed her good night, kissed the dim, far, murmuring "good night" on her own little lips. But if the child slept, they two now could not sleep.

As they lay there in the darkness, every now and then he would feel her leave her bed; he would divine her whiteness slipping across to the little girl's room; he would strain, listening as she was in there; his heart would extravagantly ease as she returned.

"Why do you do that?" he said, at length. "You mustn't do that. Why do you do that?"

She murmured: "I can't help it. I am afraid."

"When you go in there she's always there, isn't she? She's never gone, is she? She's always there. Then why do you do it? She's always there, isn't she?"

But she whispered, so low that she seemed to have sunk beneath the ground: "Oh, John—oh, John—suppose in the morning, when we went to look, she shouldn't—"

And by the sudden aching jump his heart gave he knew that fear had been seeping into him.

But this was intolerable. And mad. "Come," he said, "let's get up. Let's get out of this."

They rose and went into the living-room and flashed up all the lights. He drew in some wood from the pile outside, and he made a fire on the hearth. She got the coffeepot and placed its round cheek against the fire.

There they sat, as the night ticked by, before the fire. He tormented it with his poker; she poured coffee in the cups. There they sat, doing those things, but especially listening—listening to the light, light breathing that came in from the little back room, with its door open upon the big lighted one.

Once they relaxed. The mother looked at him, saw him, saw herself. She smiled. "You would think," she said, "we were watching over someone ill."

"Yes," he said, "we're utterly foolish."

"You know what we *are* doing, don't you?" he said, after a moment.

"Well, we are sitting here, guarding her from a small boy in Mars!"

"We're mad," she said almost laughing.

"Altogether," he agreed.

And then their hearts abruptly froze. Clare was speaking, there within the little back room: "Yes, little boy; yes, yes."

And then, "No, little boy; oh, no! Not *this* time!"

The mother sprang to her feet and rushed into the room, but Cowdray remained where he was, palsied. She returned. "She has been dreaming," she said. "She had tossed herself nearly out of her bed. I tucked her in. She's sleeping."

And the night went on as before. They replenished the fire; they stirred it; they said a few words now and then, but always they listened.

Finally they became conscious of the fact that their weary eyes were staring at windows white with dawn. They rose and shook themselves; they looked at each other's pale, lined faces and smiled.

"*What* a night! *Perfectly* mad we are!"

When, later, Cowdray set out with his canvases for the Round Beach little Clare thought she would go along a ways. "I'll walk a little ways with you along the trail, Father," she said. "I'll be right back, Mother."

They went down the winding path, through the chaparral of wild lilac and old-man. When it had become quite secluded and wild the little girl spoke: "You know, Daddy, the little boy. The little boy that spoke to me in the radio last night. The one who lives so far in a star."

"Yes. Well?"

"He came for me last night, Daddy. But I couldn't go with him—not yet. I said I wanted to stay with you and Mama.

"And you know Sleepy Eyes, the mother cat.

"The other day she ran up and down, and up, down, the trees, and then she came back to her kittens, and her fur was all sweet with this."

She crushed a fragrant leaf between her little fingers, and gave it to her father.

"We'll never know," he was thinking, "we'll never surely know."

"The reality and the dream—it's all one with a child. The real and the make-believe. They merge, they interpenetrate. We'll never know; we'll never be sure."

And that night, as they sat again in the cottage and watched small Clare playing at their feet, and once more the strange dolorous tenderness swelled their hearts, swelled their hearts, swelled their hearts, he said:

"You know, we should go back to the big cities. We are becoming absurd here."

"Oh, yes, let's go back to the big cities!" she cried and sprang to her feet.

She could see great stone houses, thousands and
thousands of them. They made great walls, they
shielded, they were great barricades. And people,
millions and millions, on all sides, tight, guarding
armies. Walls and people, impenetrable—you felt safe.
Out here—you were on the verge—on the verge—
"Oh, yes," she cried, "let us go back to the cities!"

THE QUEEN OF SPADES

By Alexander Sergeievitch Poushkin

At the house of Naroumov, a cavalry officer, the long winter night had been passed in gambling. At five in the morning breakfast was served to the weary players. The winners ate with relish; the losers, on the contrary, pushed back their plates and sat brooding gloomily. Under the influence of the good wine, however, the conversation then became general.

"Well, Sourine?" said the host inquiringly.

"Oh, I lost as usual. My luck is abominable. No matter how cool I keep, I never win."

"How is it, Herman, that you never touch a card?" remarked one of the men, addressing a young officer of the Engineering Corps. "Here you are with the rest of us at five o'clock in the morning, and you have neither played nor bet all night."

"Play interests me greatly," replied the person addressed, "but I hardly care to sacrifice the necessaries of life for uncertain superfluities."

"Herman is a German, therefore economical; that explains it," said Tomsky. "But the person I can't quite understand is my grandmother, the Countess Anna Fedorovna."

"Why?" inquired a chorus of voices.

"I can't understand why my grandmother never gambles."

"I don't see anything very striking in the fact that a woman of eighty refuses to gamble," objected Naroumov.

"Have you never heard her story?"

"No."

"Well, then, listen to it. To begin with, sixty years ago my grandmother went to Paris, where she was all the fashion. People crowded each other in the streets to get a chance to see the 'Muscovite Venus,' as she was called. All the great ladies played faro, then. On one occasion, while playing with the Duke of Orleans, she lost an enormous sum. She told her husband of the debt, but he refused outright to pay it. Nothing could induce him to change his mind on the subject, and grandmother was at her wits' ends. Finally, she remembered a friend of hers, Count Saint-Germain. You must have heard of him, as many wonderful stories have been told about him. He is said to have discovered the elixir of life, the philosopher's stone, and many other equally marvelous things. He had money at his disposal, and my grandmother knew it. She sent him a note asking him to come to see her. He obeyed her summons and found her in great distress. She painted the cruelty of her husband in the darkest colors, and ended by telling the Count that she depended upon his friendship and generosity.

"'I could lend you the money,' replied the Count, after a moment of thoughtfulness, 'but I know that you would not enjoy a moment's rest until you had returned it; it would only add to your embarrassment. There is another way of freeing yourself.'

"'But I have no money at all,' insisted my grandmother.

"'There is no need of money. Listen to me.'

"The Count then told her a secret which any of us would give a good deal to know."

The young gamesters were all attention. Tomsky lit his pipe, took a few whiffs, then continued:

"The next evening grandmother appeared at Versailles at the Queen's gaming-table. The Duke of Orleans was the dealer. Grandmother made some excuse for not having brought any money, and began to punt. She chose three cards in succession, again and again, winning every time, and was soon out of debt."

"A fable," remarked Herman; "perhaps the cards were marked."

"I hardly think so," replied Tomsky, with an air of importance.

"So you have a grandmother who knows three winning cards, and you haven't found out the magic secret."

"I must say I have not. She had four sons, one of them being my father, all of whom are devoted to play; she never told the secret to one of them. But my uncle told me this much, on his word of honor. Tchaplitzky, who died in poverty after having squandered millions, lost at one time, at play, nearly three hundred thousand rubles. He was desperate and grandmother took pity on him. She told him the three cards, making him swear never to use them again. He returned to the game, staked fifty thousand rubles on each card, and came out ahead, after paying his debts."

As day was dawning the party now broke up, each one draining his glass and taking his leave.

.   .   .   .

The Countess Anna Fedorovna was seated before her mirror in her dressing-room. Three women were assisting at her toilet. The old Countess no longer made the slightest pretensions to beauty, but she still clung to all the habits of her youth, and spent as much time at her toilet as she had done sixty years before. At the window a young girl, her ward, sat at her needlework.

"Good afternoon, grandmother," cried a young officer, who had just entered the room. "I have come to ask a favor of you."

"What, Pavel?"

"I want to be allowed to present one of my friends to you, and to take you to the ball on Tuesday night."

"Take me to the ball and present him to me there."

After a few more remarks the officer walked up to the window where Lisaveta Ivanovna sat.

"Whom do you wish to present?" asked the girl.

"Naroumov; do you know him?"

"No; is he a soldier?"

"Yes."

"An engineer?"

"No; why do you ask?"

The girl smiled and made no reply.

Pavel Tomsky took his leave, and, left to herself, Lisaveta glanced out of the window. Soon, a young officer appeared at the corner of the street; the girl blushed and bent her head low over her canvas.

This appearance of the officer had become a daily occurrence. The man was totally unknown to her, and as she was not accustomed to coquetting with the soldiers she saw on the street, she hardly knew how to explain his presence. His persistence finally roused an interest entirely strange to her. One day, she even ventured to smile upon her admirer, for such he seemed to be.

The reader need hardly be told that the officer was no other than Herman, the would-be gambler, whose imagination had been strongly excited by the story told by Tomsky of the three magic cards.

"Ah," he thought, "if the old Countess would only reveal the secret to me. Why not try to win her good-will and appeal to her sympathy?"

With this idea in mind, he took up his daily station before the house, watching the pretty face at the window, and trusting to fate to bring about the desired acquaintance.

One day, as Lisaveta was standing on the pavement about to enter the carriage after the Countess, she felt herself jostled and a note was thrust into her hand. Turning, she saw the young officer at her elbow. As quick as thought, she put the note in her glove and entered the carriage. On her return from the drive, she hastened to her chamber to read the missive, in a state of excitement mingled with fear. It was a tender and respectful declaration of affection, copied word for word from a German novel. Of this fact, Lisa was, of course, ignorant.

The young girl was much impressed by the missive, but she felt that the writer must not be encouraged. She therefore wrote a few lines of explanation and, at the first opportunity, dropped it, with the letter, out of the window. The officer hastily crossed the street, picked up the papers and entered a shop to read them.

In no wise daunted by this rebuff, he found the opportunity to send her another note in a few days. He received no reply, but, evidently understanding the female heart, he presevered, begging for an interview. He was rewarded at last by the following:

"To-night we go to the ambassador's ball. We shall remain until two o'clock. I can arrange for a meeting in this way. After our departure, the servants will probably all go out, or go to sleep. At half-past eleven enter the vestibule boldly, and if you see any one, inquire for the Countess; if not, ascend the stairs, turn to the left and go on until you come to a door, which opens into her bedchamber. Enter this room and behind a screen you will find another door leading to a corridor; from this a spiral staircase leads to my sitting-room. I shall expect to find you there on my return."

Herman trembled like a leaf as the appointed hour drew near. He obeyed instructions fully, and, as he met no one, he reached the old lady's bedchamber without difficulty. Instead of going out of the small door behind the screen, however, he concealed himself in a closet to await the return of the old Countess.

The hours dragged slowly by; at last he heard the sounds of wheels. Immediately lamps were lighted and servants began moving about. Finally the old woman tottered into the room, completely exhausted. Her women removed her wraps and proceeded to get her in readiness for the night. Herman watched the proceedings with a curiosity not unmingled with superstitious fear. When at last she was attired in cap and gown, the old woman looked less uncanny than when she wore her ball-dress of blue brocade.

She sat down in an easy chair beside a table, as she was in the habit of doing before retiring, and her women withdrew. As the old lady sat swaying to and fro, seemingly oblivious to her surroundings, Herman crept out of his hiding-place.

At the slight noise the old woman opened her eyes, and gazed at the intruder with a half-dazed expression.

"Have no fear, I beg of you," said Herman, in a calm voice. "I have not come to harm you, but to ask a favor of you instead."

The Countess looked at him in silence, seemingly without comprehending him. Herman thought she might be deaf, so he puts his lips close to her ear and repeated his remark. The listener remained perfectly mute.

"You could make my fortune without its costing you anything," pleaded the young man; "only tell me the three cards which are sure to win, and—"

Herman paused as the old woman opened her lips as if about to speak.

"It was only a jest; I swear to you, it was only a jest," came from the withered lips.

"There was no jesting about it. Remember Tchaplitzky, who, thanks to you, was able to pay his debts."

An expression of interior agitation passed over the face of the old woman; then she relapsed into her former apathy.

"Will you tell me the names of the magic cards, or not?" asked Herman after a pause.

There was no reply.

The young man then drew a pistol from his pocket, exclaiming: "You old witch, I'll force you to tell me!"

At the sight of the weapon the Countess gave a second sign of life. She threw back her head and put out her hands as if to protect herself; then they dropped and sat motionless.

Herman grasped her arm roughly, and was about to renew his threats, when he saw that she was dead!

. . . .

Seated in her room, still in her ball-dress, Lisaveta gave herself up to her reflections. She had expected to find the young officer there, but she felt relieved to see that he was not.

Strangely enough, that very night at the ball, Tomsky

had rallied her about her preference for the young officer, assuring her that he knew more than she supposed he did.

"Of whom are you speaking?" she had asked in alarm, fearing her adventure had been discovered.

"Of the remarkable man," was the reply. "His name is Herman."

Lisa made no reply.

"This Herman," continued Tomsky, "is a romantic character; he has the profile of a Napoleon and the heart of a Mephistopheles. It is said he has at least three crimes on his conscience. But how pale you are."

"It is only a slight headache. But why do you talk to me of this Herman?"

"Because I believe he has serious intentions concerning you."

"Where has he seen me?"

"At church, perhaps, or on the street."

The conversation was interrupted at this point, to the great regret of the young girl. The words of Tomsky made a deep impression upon her, and she realized how imprudently she had acted. She was thinking of all this and a great deal more when the door of her apartment suddenly opened, and Herman stood before her. She drew back at sight of him, trembling violently.

"Where have you been?" she asked in a frightened whisper.

"In the bedchamber of the Countess. She is dead," was the calm reply.

"My God! What are you saying?" cried the girl.

"Furthermore, I believe that I was the cause of her death."

The words of Tomsky flashed through Lisa's mind. Herman sat down and told her all. She listened with a feeling of terror and disgust. So those passionate letters, that audacious pursuit, were not the result of tenderness and love. It was money that he desired. The poor girl felt that she had in a sense been an accomplice in the death of her benefactress. She began to weep bitterly. Herman regarded her in silence.

"You are a monster!" exclaimed Lisa, drying her eyes.

"I didn't intend to kill her; the pistol was not even loaded."

"How are you going to get out of the house?" inquired Lisa. "It is nearly daylight. I intended to show you the way to a secret staircase, while the Countess was asleep, as we would have to cross her chamber. Now I am afraid to do so."

"Direct me, and I will find the way alone," replied Herman.

She gave him minute instructions and a key with which to open the street door. The young man pressed the cold, inert hand, then went out.

The death of the Countess has surprized no one, as it had long been expected. Her funeral was attended by every one of note in the vicinity. Herman mingled with the throng without attracting any special attention. After all the friends had taken their last look at the dead face, the young man approached the bier. He prostrated himself on the cold floor, and remained motionless for a long time. He rose at last with a face almost as pale as that of the corpse itself, and went up the steps to look into the casket. As he looked down it seemed to him that the rigid face returned his glance mockingly, closing one eye. He turned abruptly away, made a false step, and fell to the floor. He was picked up, and at the same moment, Lisaveta was carried out in a faint.

Herman did not recover his usual composure during the entire day. He dined alone at an out-of-the-way restaurant, and drank a great deal, in the hope of stifling his emotion. The wine only served to stimulate his imagination. He returned home and threw himself down on his bed without undressing.

During the night he awoke with a start; the moon shone into his chamber, making everything plainly visible. Some one looked in at the window, then quickly disappeared. He paid no attention to this, but soon he heard the vestibule door open. He thought it was his orderly, returning late, drunk as usual. The step was an unfamiliar one, and he heard the shuffling sound of loose slippers.

The door of his room opened, and a woman in white entered. She came close to the bed, and the terrified man recognized the Countess.

"I have come to you against my will," she said abruptly; "but I was commanded to grant your request. The tray, seven, and ace in succession are the magic cards. Twenty-four hours must elapse between the use of each card, and after the three have been used you must never play again."

The fantom then turned and walked away. Herman heard the outside door close, and again saw the form pass the window.

He rose and went out into the hall, where his orderly lay asleep on the floor. The door was closed. Finding no trace of a visitor, he returned to his room, lit his candle, and wrote down what he had just heard.

Two fixed ideas cannot exist in the brain at the same time any more than two bodies can occupy the same point in space. The tray, seven, and ace soon chased away the thoughts of the dead woman, and all other thoughts from the brain of the young officer. All his ideas merged into a single one: how to turn to advantage the secret paid for so dearly. He even thought of resigning his commission and going to Paris to force a fortune from conquered fate. Chance rescued him from his embarrassment.

Tchekalinsky, a man who had passed his whole life at cards, opened a club at St. Petersburg. His long experience secured for him the confidence of his companions, and his hospitality and genial humor conciliated society.

The gilded youth flocked around him, neglecting society, preferring the charms of faro to those of their sweethearts. Naroumov invited Herman to accompany him to the club, and the young man accepted the invitation only too willingly.

The two officers found the apartments full. Generals and statesmen played whist; young men· lounged on sofas, eating ices or smoking. In the principal salon stood a long table, at which about twenty men sat playing faro, the host of the establishment being the banker.

He was a man of about sixty, gray-haired and respectable. His ruddy face shone with genial humor; his eyes sparkled and a constant smile hovered around his lips.

Naroumov presented Herman. The host gave him a cordial handshake, begged him not to stand upon ceremony, and returned to his dealing. More than thirty cards were already on the table. Tchekalinsky paused after each coup, to allow the punters time to recognize their gains or losses, politely answering all questions and constantly smiling.

After the deal was over, the cards were shuffled and the game began again.

"Permit me to choose a card," said Herman, stretching out his hand over the head of a portly gentleman, to reach a livret. The banker bowed without replying.

Herman chose a card, and wrote the amount of his stake upon it with a piece of chalk.

"How much is that?" asked the banker; "excuse me, sir, but I do not see well."

"Forty thousand rubles," said Herman coolly.

All eyes were instantly turned upon the speaker.

"He has lost his wits," thought Naroumov.

"Allow me to observe," said Tchekalinsky, with his eternal smile, "that your stake is excessive."

"What of it?" replied Herman, nettled. "Do you accept it or not?"

The banker nodded in assent. "I have only to remind you that the cash will be necessary; of course your word is good, but in order to keep the confidence of my patrons, I prefer the ready money."

Herman took a bank-check from his pocket and handed it to his host. The latter examined it attentively, then laid it on the card chosen.

He began dealing: to the right, a nine; to the left, a tray.

"The tray wins," said Herman, showing the card he held—a tray.

A murmur ran through the crowd. Tchekalinsky frowned for a second only, then his smile returned. He took a roll of bank-bills from his pocket and counted out the required sum. Herman received it and at once left the table.

The next evening saw him at the place again. Every one eyed him curiously, and Tchekalinsky greeted him cordially.

He selected his card and placed upon it his fresh

stake. The banker began dealing: to the right, a nine; to the left, a seven.

Herman then showed his card—a seven spot. The onlookers exclaimed, and the host was visibly disturbed. He counted out ninety-four thousand rubles and passed them to Herman, who accepted them without showing the least surprise, and at once withdrew.

The following evening he went again. His appearance was the signal for the cessation of all occupation, every one being eager to watch the developments of events. He selected his card—an ace.

The dealing began: to the right, a queen; to the left, an ace.

"The ace wins," remarked Herman, turning up his card without glancing at it.

"Your queen is killed," remarked Tchekalinsky quietly.

Herman trembled; looking down, he saw, not the ace he had selected, but the queen of spades. He could scarcely believe his eyes. It seemed impossible that he could have made such a mistake. As he stared at the card it seemed to him that the queen winked one eye at him mockingly.

"The old woman!" he exclaimed involuntarily.

The croupier raked in the money while he looked on in stupid terror. When he left the table, all made way for him to pass; the cards were shuffled, and the gambling went on.

Herman became a lunatic. He was confined at the hospital at Oboukov, where he spoke to no one, but kept constantly murmuring in a monotonous tone: "The tray, seven, ace! The tray, seven, queen!"

QUALITY

By John Galsworthy

I knew him from the days of my extreme youth, because he made my father's boots; inhabiting with his elder brother two little shops let into one, in a small by-street—now no more, but then most fashionably placed in the West End.

That tenement had a certain quiet distinction; there was no sign upon its face that he made for any of the Royal Family—merely his own German name of Gessler Brothers; and in the window a few pairs of boots. I remember that it always troubled me to account for those unvarying boots in the window, for he made only what was ordered, reaching nothing down, and it failed to fit. Had he bought them to put there? That, too, seemed inconceivable. He would never have tolerated in his house leather on which he had not worked himself. Besides, they were too beautiful—the pair of pumps, so inexpressibly slim, the patent leathers with cloth tops, making water come into one's mouth, the tall brown riding-boots with marvellous sooty glow, as if, tho new, they had been worn a hundred years. Those pairs could only have been made by one who saw before him the Soul of Boot—so truly were they prototypes incarnating the very spirit of all footgear. These thoughts, of course, came to me later, tho even when I was promoted to him, at the age of per-

haps fourteen, some inkling haunted me of the dignity
of himself and brother. For to make boots—such boots
as he made—seemed to me then, and still seems to me,
mysterious and wonderful.

I remember well my shy remark, one day, while
stretching out to him my youthful foot:

"Isn't it awfully hard to do, Mr. Gessler?"

And his answer, given with a sudden smile from out
of the sardonic redness of his beard: "Id is an Ardt!"

Himself, he was a little as if made from leather, with
his yellow crinkly face, and crinkly reddish hair and
beard, and neat folds slanting down his cheeks to the
corners of his mouth, and his guttural and one-toned
voice; for leather is a sardonic substance, and stiff and
slow of purpose. And that was the character of his
face, save that his eyes, which were gray-blue had in
them the simple gravity of one secretly possessed by
the Ideal. His elder brother was so very like him—
tho watery, paler in every way, with a great indus-
try—that sometimes in early days I was not quite sure
of him until the interview was over. Then I knew that
it was he, if the words, "I will ask my brudder," had
not been spoken; and that, if they had, it was his elder
brother.

When one grew old and wild and ran up bills, one
somehow never ran them up with Gessler Brothers. It
would not have seemed becoming to go in there and
stretch out one's foot to that blue iron-spectacled
glance, owing him for more than—say—two pairs, just
the comfortable reassurance that one was still his client.

For it was not possible to go to him very often—his
boots lasted terribly, having something beyond the
temporary—some, as it were, essence of boot stitched
into them.

One went in, not as into most shops, in the mood of: "Please serve me, and let me go!" but restfully, as one enters a church; and, sitting on the single wooden chair, waited—for there was never anybody there. Soon, over the top edge of that sort of well—rather dark, and smelling soothingly of leather—which formed the shop, there would be seen his face, or that of his elder brother, peering down. A guttural sound, and the tip-tap of bast slippers beating the narrow wooden stairs, and he would stand before one without coat, a little bent, in leather apron, with sleeves turned back, blinking—as if awakened from some dream of boots, or like an owl surprized in daylight and annoyed at this interruption.

And I would say: "How do you do, Mr. Gessler? Could you make me a pair of Russia leather boots?"

Without a word he would leave me, retiring whence he came, or into the other portion of the shop, and I would continue to rest in the wooden chair, inhaling the incense of his trade. Soon he would come back, holding in his thin, veined hand a piece of gold-brown leather. With eyes fixed on it, he would remark: "What a beaudiful biece!" When I, too, had admired it, he would speak again. "When do you wand dem?" And I would answer: "Oh! As soon as you conveniently can." And he would say: "To-morrow fordnighd?" Or if he were his elder brother: "I will ask my brudder!"

Then I would murmur: "Thank you! Good-morning Mr. Gessler." "Goot-morning!" he would reply, still looking at the leather in his hand. And as I moved to the door, I would hear the tip-tap of his bast slippers restoring him, up the stairs, to his dream of boots. But if it were some new kind of footgear that he had not yet made me, then indeed he would observe ceremony—divesting me of my boot and holding it long in his hand, looking at it with eyes at once critical and loving, as if recalling the glow with which he had created it, and rebuking the way in which one had disorganized this masterpiece. Then, placing my foot on a piece of paper, he would two or three times tickle the outer edges with a pencil and pass his nervous fingers over my toes, feeling himself into the heart of my requirements.

I cannot forget that day on which I had occasion to say to him: "Mr. Gessler, that last pair of town walking-boots creaked, you know."

He looked at me for a time without replying, as if expecting me to withdraw or qualify the statement, then said:

"Id shouldn'd 'ave greaked."

"It did, I'm afraid."

"You goddem wed before dey found demselves?"

"I don't think so."

At that he lowered his eyes, as if hunting for memory of those boots, and I felt sorry I had mentioned this grave thing.

"Zend dem back!" he said; "I will look at dem."

A feeling of compassion for my creaking boots surged up in me, so well could I imagine the sorrowful long curiosity of regard which he would bend on them.

"Zome boods," he said slowly, "are bad from birdt. If I can do noding wid dem, I dake dem off your bill."

Once (once only) I went absent-mindedly into his shops in a pair of boots bought in an emergency at some large firm's. He took my order without showing me any leather, and I could feel his eyes penetrating the inferior integument of my foot. At last he said:

"Dose are nod my boods."

The tone was not one of anger, nor of sorrow, not
even of contempt, but there was in it something quiet
that froze the blood. He put his hand down and
pressed a finger on the place where the left boot, en-
deavoring to be fashionable, was not quite comfortable.

"Id 'urds you dere," he said. "Dose big virms 'ave
no self-respect. Drash!" And then, as if something
had given way within him, he spoke long and bitterly.
It was the only time I ever heard him discuss the con-
ditions and hardships of his trade.

"Dey get id all," he said, "dey get id by adverdise-
ment, nod by work. Dey dake it away from us, who
lofe our boods. Id gomes to this—bresently I haf no
work. Every year id gets less—you will see." And
looking at his lined face I saw things I had never
noticed before, bitter things and bitter struggle—and
what a lot of gray hairs there seemed suddenly in his
red beard!

As best I could, I explained the circumstances of the
purchase of those ill-omened boots. But his face and
voice made a so deep impression that during the next
few minutes I ordered many pairs. Nemesis fell!
They lasted more terribly than ever. And I was not
able conscientiously to go to him for nearly two years.

When at last I went I was surprised to find that
outside one of the two little windows of his shop another name was painted, also that of a bootmaker—
making, of course, for the Royal Family. The old
familiar boots, no longer in dignified isolation, were
huddled in the single window. Inside, the now con-
tracted well of the one little shop was more scented
and darker than ever. And it was longer than usual,
too, before a face peered down, and the tip-tap of the

bast slippers began. At last he stood before me, and, gazing through those rusty iron spectacles, said:

"Mr.——, isn'd it?"

"Ah! Mr. Gessler," I stammered, "but your boots are really *too* good, you know! See, these are quite decent still!" And I stretched out to him my foot. He looked at it.

"Yes," he said, "beople do nod wand good boods, id seems."

To get away from his reproachful eyes and voice I hastily remarked: "What have you done to your shop?"

He answered quietly: "Id was too exbensif. Do you wand some boods?"

I ordered three pairs, tho I had only wanted two, and quickly left. I had, I know not quite what feeling of being part, in his mind, of a conspiracy against him; or not perhaps so much against him as against his idea of boot. One does not, I suppose, care to feel like that; for it was again many months before my next visit to his shop, paid, I remember, with the feeling: "Oh! well, I can't leave the old boy—so here goes! Perhaps it'll be his elder brother!"

For his elder brother, I knew, had not character enough to reproach me, even dumbly.

And, to my relief, in the shop there did appear to be his elder brother, handling a piece of leather.

"Well, Mr. Gessler," I said, "how are you?"

He came close, and peered at me.

"I am breddy well," he said slowly; "but my elder brudder is dead."

And I saw that it was indeed himself—but how aged and wan! And never before had I heard him mention his brother. Much shocked, I murmured: "Oh! I am sorry!"

"Yes," he answered, "he was a good man, he made a good bood; but he is dead." And he touched the top of his head, where the hair had suddenly gone as thin as it had been on that of his poor brother, to indicate, I suppose, the cause of death. "He could nod ged over losing do oder shop. Do you wand any boods?" And he held up the leather in his hand: "Id's a beaudiful biece."

I ordered several pairs. It was very long before they came—but they were better than ever. One simply could not wear them out. And soon after that I went abroad.

It was over a year before I was again in London. And the first shop I went to was my old friend's. I had left a man of sixty, I came back to one of seventy-five, pinched and worn and tremulous, who genuinely, this time, did not at first know me.

"Oh! Mr. Gessler," I said, sick at heart; "how splendid your boots are! See, I've been wearing this pair nearly all the time I've been abroad; and they're not halfworn out, are they?"

He looked long at my boots—a pair of Russia leather, and his face seemed to regain steadiness. Putting his hand on my instep, he said:

"Do dey vid you here? I 'ad drouble wid dat bair, I remember."

I assured him that they had fitted beautifully.

"Do you wand any boods?" he said. "I can make dem quickly; id is a slack dime."

I answered: "Please, please! I want boots all round —every kind!"

"I will make a vresh model. Your food must be bigger." And with utter slowness, he traced round my foot, and felt my toes, only once looking up to say:

"Did I dell you my brudder was dead?"

To watch him was painful, so feeble had he grown; I was glad to get away.

I had given those boots up, when one evening they came. Opening the parcel, I set the four pairs out in a row. Then one by one I tried them on. There was no doubt about it. In shape and fit, in finish and quality of leather, they were the best he had ever made me. And in the mouth of one of the town walking-boots I found his bill. The amount was the same as usual, but it gave me quite a shock. He had never before sent it in till quarter day. I flew downstairs and wrote a check, and posted it at once with my own hand.

A week later, passing the little street, I thought I would go in and tell him how splendidly the new boots fitted. But when I came to where his shop had been, his name was gone. Still there, in the window, were the slim pumps, the patent leathers with cloth tops, the sooty riding-boots.

I went in, very much disturbed. In the two little shops—again made into one—was a young man with an English face.

"Mr. Gessler in?" I said.

He gave me a strange, ingratiating look.

"No, sir," he said, "no. But we can attend to anything with pleasure. We've taken the shop over. You've seen our name, no doubt, next door. We make for some very good people."

"Yes, yes," I said; "but Mr. Gessler?"

"Oh!" he answered; "dead."

"Dead! But I only received these boots from him last Wednesday week."

"Ah!" he said; "a shockin' go. Poor old man starved 'imself."

"Good God!"

"Slow starvation, the doctor called it! You see he went to work in such a way! Would keep the shop on; wouldn't have a soul touch his boots except himself. When he got an order, it took him such a time. People won't wait. He lost everybody. And there he'd sit, goin' on and on——I will say that for him——not a man in London made a better boot! But look at the competition! He never advertized! Would 'ave the best leather, too, and do it all 'imself. Well, there it is. What could you expect with his ideas?"

"But starvation——!"

"That may be a bit flowery, as the sayin' is——but I know myself he was sittin' over his boots day and night, to the very last. You see I used to watch him. Never gave 'imself time to eat; never had a penny in the house. All went in rent and leather. How he lived so long I don't know. He regular let his fire go out. He was a character. But he made good boots."

"Yes," I said, "he made good boots."